"These guys are persistent. I'll give them that."

"Which means we can't go to the next ranger station. They'll be waiting for us there." If they weren't already. Vincent couldn't take the chance. Not after Shea had risked her life to save his. He'd promised to get her to New York to fight for her son, and he had no intention of failing her again. "We have to go deeper into the woods. North. They won't be looking for us there."

"Every minute we spend out here is another chance we don't make it out of these mountains." Wide eyes searched his face. "If we head north, we'll just be saving the guys with the guns the trouble when we die out here from exposure."

"We have to take the risk. Otherwise, they'll shoot us on sight. I need you to trust me."

THE LINE
OF DUTY

NICHOLE SEVERN

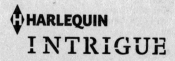

This one's for you! You made this series possible, and while this might be the last book of the origin series, Blackhawk Security isn't finished yet!

Recycling programs
for this product may
not exist in your area.

ISBN-13: 978-1-335-13677-0

The Line of Duty

Copyright © 2020 by Natascha Jaffa

This edition published by arrangement with Harlequin Books S.A.

For questions and comments about the quality of this book, please contact us at CustomerService@Harlequin.com.

Harlequin Enterprises ULC
22 Adelaide St. West, 40th Floor
Toronto, Ontario M5H 4E3, Canada
www.Harlequin.com

Printed in U.S.A.

Nichole Severn writes explosive romantic suspense with strong heroines, heroes who dare challenge them and a hell of a lot of guns. She resides with her very supportive and patient husband, as well as her demon spawn, in Utah. When she's not writing, she's constantly injuring herself running, rock climbing, practicing yoga and snowboarding. She loves hearing from readers through her website, www.nicholesevern.com, and on Facebook, www.Facebook.com/nichole.severn.

Books by Nichole Severn

Harlequin Intrigue

Blackhawk Security

Rules in Blackmail
Rules in Rescue
Rules in Deceit
Rules in Defiance
Caught in the Crossfire
The Line of Duty

Midnight Abduction

Visit the Author Profile page at Harlequin.com.

CAST OF CHARACTERS

Vincent Kalani—Blackhawk Security's forensics expert Vincent Kalani has a lead in the investigation into who tried to kill him while he was working for the NYPD a year ago. Only with each piece of evidence recovered and the people responsible closing in, he realizes he's the one putting his Anchorage PD partner in more danger.

Shea Ramsey—Shea Ramsey will do anything to get custody of her son back from her ex. As one of Anchorage PD's finest officers and a consultant for Blackhawk Security, she's fighting to make up for the past, but when she's pulled into a killer's sights, she fears not even Vincent can save her.

Lara Richards—Vincent's former superior officer is ready to end the fight that forced her best forensic investigator into hiding. She's been looking into a group of suspects on her own, and what she's found is going to change the entire course of the investigation.

Blackhawk Security—Comprised of an elite team of specialists with diverse backgrounds ranging from ex–special forces to psychology, Blackhawk Security operatives offer close, personal protective services for people whose lives are endangered and for each other.

Chapter One

He had a lead.

The partial fingerprint he'd lifted from the murder scene hadn't been a partial at all, but evidence of a severe burn on the owner's index finger that altered the print. He hadn't been able to get an ID with so few markers to compare before leaving New York City a year ago. But now, Blackhawk Security forensic expert Vincent Kalani finally had a chance to bring down a killer.

He hauled his duffel bag higher on his shoulder. He had to get back to New York, convince his former commanding officer to reopen the case. His muscles burned under the weight as he ducked beneath the small passenger plane's wing and climbed inside. Cold Alaskan air drove beneath his heavy coat, but catching sight of the second passenger already aboard chased back the chill.

"Shea Ramsey." Long, curly dark hair slid over her shoulder as jade-green eyes widened in surprise. His entire body nearly gave in to the increased sense of gravity pulling at him had it not been for the paralysis working through his muscles. Officer Shea Ramsey had assisted Blackhawk Security with investigations in the past at the insistence of Anchorage's chief of police, but her formfitting pair of jeans, T-shirt and zip-up hoodie announced she wasn't here on business. Hell, she was a damn beautiful woman, an even better investigator and apparently headed to New York. Same as him. "Anchorage Police Department's finest, indeed."

"What the hell are you doing here?" Shea shuffled her small backpack at her feet, crossing her arms over her midsection. The tendons between her shoulders and neck corded with tension as she stared out her side of the plane. No mistaking the bitterness in her voice. "Is Blackhawk following me now?"

"Should we be?" Blackhawk Security provided top-of-the-line security measures for their exclusive clientele, including cameras, body-heat sensors, motion detectors and more. Whatever their clients needed, Sullivan Bishop and his team delivered. Personal protection, network security, private investigating, logistical support to the US government and personal recovery. They even had their very own profiler on staff to aid the FBI with serial cases. The firm did it all. Vincent mainly headed the forensics division, but he'd take up any case with Shea's involvement in a heartbeat. His gut tightened. Hard to ignore the quiet strength she'd kept close to the vest when they partnered together on these past few cases. It'd pulled him in, made him want to get to know her more, but she'd only met him—and every member of his team— with resentment. Not all Anchorage PD officers agreed with the partnership between the city and the most prestigious security firm in Alaska. Officer Ramsey led that charge.

He shoved his duffel into the cargo area as the pilot maneuvered into his seat. The small plane bounced with the movement. The cabin, he couldn't help but notice, filled with her scent. "I'm not here on Blackhawk business. I've got…personal business to take care of in New York. You?"

"I have a life outside of the department." She hadn't turned to look at him, her knuckles white through the taut skin of her hands as she gripped the seat's arms. The plane's engine growled at the push of a button, rotors sending vibrations through the sardine can meant to get them halfway to New York in one piece before they switched to another aircraft to make the rest of the trip.

"You guys ready?" the pilot asked. "Here are your headsets."

Hell, Shea was so tense as she took hers, she probably thought the wrong gust of wind could shoot them out of the sky. She closed her eyes, muscles working hard in her throat. The tarmac attendants removed the heavy rubber blocks from around the plane's wheels, and they slowly rolled forward. Every muscle down her spine seemed to further tighten.

Something inside him felt for her, forced him to reach out to offer assurance. Vincent positioned the headset over his ears, then slid his hand on top of hers. Smooth skin caught on the calluses in his palms, and suddenly those green eyes were on him. In an instant, her fingers tangled with his. Heat exploded through him, the breath rushing out of his lungs as she gripped on to him as though her life depended on it.

Pressure built behind his sternum as the small passenger plane raced down the runway, then climbed higher into the sky. His back pressed into the soft leather seats, but his attention focused 100 percent on the woman beside him. On the way her skin remained stretched along her forearm revealing the map of veins below, on the unsteady rising and falling of her shoulders when she breathed. Snow-capped mountains disappeared below the windows, only reappearing as the plane leveled out high above the peaks mere minutes later. The pilot directed them toward the mountains, but the pressure hadn't released from his rib cage. Not when Shea was still holding on to him so tightly. He raised his voice over the sound of the engine. "I'm going to need that hand back sooner or later."

"Right. Sorry." Shea released her grip, then wiped her palm down her thigh, running the same hand through her curly hair. Her voice barely registered above the noise around them. "You'd think five years on the job would give me a little more backbone when it came to planes."

"There's a difference between facing the bad guys and facing our fears." His hand was still warm from where their skin had made contact, and he curled his fingers into his palm to hold on to it for as long as he could. "At least there was for me."

She slid that beautiful gaze to his, the freckles dusted across the bridge of her nose and onto her cheeks more pronounced than a few minutes ago. "You were with NYPD's forensics unit for nine years before you came out here, right? Can't imagine there's much that scares you anymore."

She'd be surprised. Her words slowly sank in over the engine's mid-frequency drone, and Vincent narrowed his attention. She'd looked into him. There was no way she could've known how long he'd worked forensics by simply searching for him on the internet. NYPD records weren't public information. Which meant she'd used her access through federal databases. Out of curiosity? Or something else? His attention darted to his duffel bag. He'd booked a private passenger plane out of Merrill Field for a reason. The SIG SAUER P226 with twelve deadly rounds of ammo in the magazine was currently nestled in his bag. He'd worked with Officer Ramsey before. The background check the firm had run on her when Blackhawk had need of the department's assistance on past investigations hadn't connected her with anyone from his past. But what were the chances that she of all people had ended up on this flight? "Someone's been doing their homework."

"All of you Blackhawk Security types are the same. You take the law into your own hands and don't care if you jeopardize the department's cases. You run your own investigations, then expect officers like me to clean up your mess. You're vigilantes, and you endanger the people in this city every time you step out of your downtown highrise office. So, yes, I've done my homework. I like to know who I'm being forced to work with." She pinned him to his seat with that green gaze, and the world disappeared around them. "And you… you were a cop. You used to have a conscience."

Vincent clenched his back teeth against the fire

exploding through him. He leaned into her, ensuring she couldn't look away this time. "You have no idea—"

The plane jerked downward, throwing his heart into his throat. The engine choked, then started up again. He locked his attention out through the plane's windshield. His pulse beat loudly behind his ears. The rotors were slowing, grinding. He shouldn't have been able to track a single propeller if they were running at the right speed. Gripping one hand around his seat's arm, he pressed his shoulders into the leather and shouted into his mic. "What the hell is going on?"

"I don't know." The pilot shot his hand to the instrument panel. "We're losing altitude fast, but all of the gauges check out." Wrapping his hand around the plane's handheld CB radio, the pilot raised his voice over the protests of the engine. "Mayday, Mayday, Mayday. Merrill Field, this is Captain Reginald, a Robin DR400, Delta-Echo, Lima, Juliet, Golf, with total engine failure attempting forced landing. Last known position seven miles east of Anchorage; 1,500 feet heading ninety degrees." Static filled their headsets. "Can anybody read me?" The pilot looked back at his passengers. "The controls aren't responding! I'm going to have to try to put her down manually!"

Vincent pressed his hand to the window and

searched the ridges and valleys below for a safe place they could land. Nothing but pure white snow and miles of mountains. Jagged peaks, trees. There was no way they'd survive a forced landing here. There were no safe places to land.

"No, no, no. No! This wasn't supposed to happen." The panic in Shea's voice flooded his veins with ice. She grabbed her backpack off the floor from between her feet and clutched it to her chest. Fear showed brightly in her eyes a split second before she was thrown back in her seat. She clutched the window. "This wasn't supposed to happen."

The engine smoked, and the plane jerked again. Vincent slammed into the side door. Pain ricocheted through the side of his head, but he forced it to the back of his mind. They were losing altitude fast, and dizziness gripped him hard. They had to get the engine back up and running, or they were all going to die. He couldn't breathe, couldn't think. Double-checking his seat belt, Vincent locked on Shea's terrified features. *This wasn't supposed to happen*. The mountain directly outside her window edged closer. "Watch out!"

Metal met rock in an ear-piercing screech. The mountain cut into the side of the plane, taking the right wing, then caught on the back stabilizer and ripped off the tail end. Cold Alaska air rushed into the cabin as luggage and supplies vanished into the wilderness. The plane rocked to one side, the ground coming up to meet them faster than Vincent expected. He dug his fingers into the leather armrest, every muscle in his body tensed.

The pilot's voice echoed through the cabin. "Brace for impact!"

He reached out for Shea. "Hang on!"

THE SKY WAS on fire.

Red streaks bled into purple on one side and green on the other as she stared out the small window to her right, stars prickling through the auroras she'd fallen in love with the very first night she'd come to Anchorage. Rocky peaks and trees framed her vision, and every cell in her body flooded with pain in an instant. A groan caught in Shea Ramsey's throat, the weight on her chest blocking precious oxygen. Her feet were numb. How long had she been unconscious? Her hands shook as she tested the copilot seat weighing on her sternum. Closing her eyes against the agony, she put everything she had into getting out from under the hunk of metal and leather, but it wouldn't budge.

The plane had gone down, Vincent's shout so loud in her head. And then… Shea pushed at the debris again as panic clawed through her. They'd crashed in the mountains. The pilot hadn't been able to reach anyone on the radio. Did anyone even know they were out here? She couldn't breathe. Tears prickled at the corners of her eyes as the remains of the plane came into focus. Along with the unconscious man in the seat beside her. "Vincent, can you hear me?"

His long black hair covered the pattern of tattoos inked into his arms and neck as well as his overly attractive face. His Hawaiian heritage and that body of a powerful demigod had tugged at something primal within her every time she was forced to work alongside him in the field, but she'd buried that feeling deep. He shouldn't have been here. The pilot had told her she'd be the only passenger on this flight. She hadn't meant for the Blackhawk Security operative to get involved—hadn't meant anyone to get involved—but she'd been so desperate to get to New York. That same determination tore through her now as the plane jerked a few more inches along the snowbank. Out Vincent's window it looked like they'd crashed at the base of a steep cliffside, with nothing but sky and snow in every direction. A scream escaped her throat as the cabin shook. One wrong move would send them down the short slope and over the edge.

"Shea." A groan reached her ears as Vincent stirred in his seat. Locking soothing brown eyes on her through the trail of blood snaking through his left eyebrow, he pushed his hair back with one hand. "That…did not go as I expected. But we're okay. It's going to be okay."

Was he trying to convince her or himself?

"I can't…breathe." Understanding lit his bearded features as he noted the seat pressing against her chest, and in that moment, her body heat spiked with the concern sliding into his expression. Memory of him holding her hand during takeoff rushed to the front of her mind. Vincent pushed out of his seat, and the plane slid another couple of inches toward the cliff. She closed her eyes as terror ricocheted through her. "No, don't!"

"Shea, look at me." His featherlight touch trailed down her jaw, and she forced herself to follow his command. He stilled, bending at the knees until her gaze settled on his. Her heart pounded hard at the base of her skull but slowed the longer he stared at her. "I'm going to get you out of here, okay? You have my word. I need you to trust me."

Trust him. The people he worked for—worked with—couldn't be trusted. None of them could. Blackhawk Security might help catch the bad guys, same as her, but at the cost of breaking the law she'd taken an oath to uphold. They didn't deserve her trust, but the pain in her chest wouldn't let up, was getting worse, and all she could do was nod.

He moved forward slowly, and Shea strengthened her grip on the metal crushing her. The only reason the seat hadn't killed her was because of the padded backpack she'd clutched before the crash, but how much more could her body take? The plane was shifting again, threatening to slide right toward another cliff edge. They'd survived a crash landing from 1,500 feet. What were the chances they'd survive another? Vincent crouched beside her, the plane barely large enough to contain his hulking size. Although the gaping hole at the tail end helped. "Hey, eyes on me, Officer. Nowhere else, you got that? I'm going to try to get this thing off of you, but I need you to focus on me."

Focus on him. She could do that. She'd spent so long trying not to notice him while they worked their joint investigations, it was a nice change to have permission for once. Pins and needles spread through her feet and hands as cold worked deep into her bones. The back of the plane had been separated from the main fuselage, and the bloodied windshield had a large hole where she'd expected to see the pilot in his seat. They were in the middle of the Alaskan wilderness, and temperatures were dropping by the minute. "You're…bleeding."

"I've survived worse." He skimmed his fingers over hers, and her awareness of how close he'd gotten rocketed her heart into her throat.

"Worse than…a plane crash?" How was that

possible? She'd read his service records, thanks to a former partner now working for the NYPD. Vincent Kalani had been assigned to the department's Detective Bureau's Forensic Investigations Division, collecting and analyzing evidence from crime scenes for close to ten years. Until suddenly he wasn't. There was nothing in those files about an injury in the line of duty. In fact, it was as though he'd simply disappeared before signing on with Sullivan Bishop's new security firm here in Anchorage.

"I think I've got this loose enough to move it. You ready? I need you to push the seat forward as hard as you can." Vincent handled the leather seat crushing her chest. "On my count. One, two, three." Together, they shoved the debris forward, and Shea gasped as much crisp, clean air as her lungs allowed.

"Thank you." The pain vanished as he maneuvered the hunk of metal to the front of the plane, and a panicked laugh bubbled to the surface. Because if she didn't have this small release, Shea feared she might break down here in front of him. The ground rumbled beneath them, and she stilled. The plane hadn't moved. At least, not as far as she could tell. So what—

Another shock wave rolled through the fuselage, and she tightened her grip around the backpack in her lap. "Vincent..."

Fear cut through the relief that'd spread over his expression. "Avalanche."

Shea twisted in her seat, staring up at the ripples creasing through the snowbanks high above, her fingers plastered against the window. Strong hands ripped her out of her seat and thrust her toward the back of the plane. Adrenaline flooded into her veins, triggering her fight-or-flight response. The plane tilted to one side as they raced toward the back, threatening to roll with their escape. Cargo slid into her path. Her boot caught on a black duffel bag, and she hit freezing metal. The rumble was growing louder outside, stronger.

"Go, go, go!" Vincent helped her to her feet, keeping close on her heels as the plane shifted beneath them. With a final push, he forced her through the hole where the tail end of the plane was supposed to be, but they couldn't stop. Not with an entire mountain of snow cascading directly toward them.

Flakes worked into the tops of her boots and soaked through her jeans. She pumped her legs as hard as she could, but it wouldn't be enough. The avalanche was moving too fast. She was going to die out here, and everything she'd worked for—

everything she'd ever cared about—wouldn't matter anymore.

"There!" Vincent fisted her jacket and shoved her ahead of him. "Head for that opening!"

Trying to gain control of the panic eating her alive from the inside, Shea sprinted as fast as several feet of snow would let her toward what looked like the entrance to a cave a mere twenty feet ahead of them. Her fingers ached from the grip she kept on the backpack, but it was nothing compared to the burn in her lungs. A rush of cold air and flecks of snow blew her hair into her face and disrupted her vision, but she wouldn't stop. Couldn't stop. Ten feet. Five. She pumped her free arm to gain momentum. Sweat beaded at the base of her neck. They were going to make it. They *had* to make it. Glancing back over her shoulder, she ensured Vincent was still behind her, but the plane had already been consumed. Snow started to fall over the cave's entrance in a thundering rush, and she lunged for the opening before it disappeared completely.

And hit solid dirt.

She clutched the backpack close to her chest, as if it'd bring any kind of comfort.

Within seconds, darkness filled her vision, only the sound of her and Vincent's combined breathing registering over the rumble of them being buried alive. She reached for him, skimming her finger-tips across what she assumed was one of his arms, but the padding of his jacket was too thick to be sure. Dust filled her nostrils as she fought to catch her breath. Silence descended, the wall of snow and ice settling over the cave. "You saved my life."

A soft hissing sound preceded a burst of orange flame. Shadows danced over Vincent's features, his battle-worn expression on full display in the dull flame of the lighter, and a hint of the awareness she'd felt when he'd held her hand during takeoff settled low in her stomach. Faster than she thought possible, he hauled her from the floor and pinned her against the wall of the cave and his body with one hand, her pack forgotten. "Tell me why you were on that plane."

His body pressed into hers. Shadowed, angry angles were carved into his features, unlike anything she'd seen before when they'd worked together. Shea pushed at him, but he was so much stronger, so much bigger. "Get off me."

"Before we crashed you said, 'This wasn't supposed to happen.'" He increased the pressure at the base of her throat, simulating the crushing debris he'd pulled off her chest mere minutes ago. "There was no reason that plane should've crashed unless it'd been sabotaged. You know something, and I'm not letting you go until you tell me who sent you after me—"

Turning one side of her body into him, she struck his forearm with the base of her palm and withdrew her service weapon with her free hand from the shoulder holster beneath her jacket. She aimed center mass, just as she'd been trained, but kept her finger alongside the trigger. "Touch me again and I won't hesitate to shoot you. Understand?"

He backed off, easing the blood pulsing in her face and neck.

"Nobody sent me after you, whatever the hell that means." In the dim light of the flame, Shea swallowed the discomfort in her throat as though that would make it easier to breathe, but she wouldn't lower her weapon. "I was on the plane because I need to get my son back."

Chapter Two

"What do you mean get him back?" Shea had a son. Of all the cases they'd worked together, neither of them had revealed more than they'd had to, but a son? Why hadn't that come up in her background check? How hadn't he known, and why did the thought of her creating life with another man tear at the edges of the hollowness inside him?

She lowered the barrel of her service weapon an inch, but kept the gun raised. Like the strong, stubborn, suspicious police officer he'd come to know. He shouldn't have pinned her against the wall, her sultry scent embedded now in his lungs. But more than that, he hadn't meant to intimidate her. Hadn't meant to drive a larger wedge between them than already existed. "My husband—my ex-husband—he..." Swiping her tongue across her bottom lip, Shea shifted her weight between both feet, but her gaze softened in the little bit of flame they had left. "He took Wells from me."

The muscles down Vincent's spine hardened with battle-ready tension. Rage, hot and fast, exploded through his veins. Her son had been taken. He could only imagine the hurt, the fear she'd had to live with this entire time, and she hadn't said a word. Every cell in his body urged him to find the bastard responsible and make him pay, to bring her son home, but there was nothing he could do for either of them right now. Sympathy flooded through him, and he raised his hands in surrender, the lighter clutched between his thumb and palm. "You can put the gun down."

One second. Two. She lowered the gun to her side but didn't holster it. Pressing her back against the cave wall, she slid to her haunches and collected the backpack she'd held on to so tightly during the flight. "Why do you think the plane was sabotaged? Flights go down all the time. It could've been an accident—"

"Because of the pilot," he said. "He reported the gauges were fine, but the engine had stalled. My guess is someone tampered with the fuel tank. Maybe replaced the fuel with some other kind of liquid. The gauge would've read full, but the engine can't run without gas."

"I didn't sabotage the plane." She nodded absently. "But I might know who did."

"Let me guess. Your ex." Hell. He'd been dispatched to enough domestic cases over the years to understand the lengths some guys went to keep their girlfriends or wives from escaping, but bringing down a plane? Kidnapping a child? Vincent forced himself to breathe evenly. Any evidence that someone had messed with the plane was gone, buried as deep as if not deeper than they were at the moment. No way to confirm Shea's ex-husband—or anyone else—was responsible, but he wouldn't discount the possibility that her being on that plane wasn't just a coincidence. "Tell me about your son."

"Wells?" Her lips tugged into a weak smile as she holstered her weapon under her jacket. Dark patches of water stained her jeans, and he realized she must be freezing right about now. The sun had already started going down when they'd woken up in the wreckage. So they'd have to make camp here tonight, get a fire going once he mapped out the rest of the cave. Maybe there was another entrance that hadn't been buried during the avalanche. "He's…a handful. Unlimited energy, great negotiation skills, even though he's not old enough to talk." A laugh escaped as she pushed her long dark hair over her head, but her smile disappeared as quickly as it come. "I found out I was pregnant a couple months after Logan and I got married. We were both so excited to be parents, but then…

then everything changed." Shadows hid her expression as Shea wiped her palms down her jeans and stood. "My ex was able to convince a judge to give him temporary custody of our son after the divorce, but I have to fight for him. Logan has been doing everything he can to keep me from seeing Wells. Sending threatening messages, having me followed, but I never thought he'd bring down a plane to keep me from getting to the custody hearing. That he would try to kill me."

Whoever was behind this had almost succeeded, too.

"That's why you were headed to New York." Hell. And they'd just crashed in the middle of the Alaskan wilderness. Vincent gripped the lighter in his hand; her gaze blazed in the dim light. They'd barely escaped with their lives and had been trapped in this cave under who knew how many feet of snow. As far as rescue coming, the tower had no idea they'd gone down, and their pilot had gone missing. Maybe had even been buried in the avalanche after getting thrown from the crash site. Vincent had taken leave from Blackhawk for the next week and a half. No one would know he hadn't made it to New York. As far as his team was concerned, he was going back home to Hawaii. So he and Shea…they weren't going anywhere. "Did you file a complaint with the police department?"

She hesitated, bottom lip parting slightly from the top, then shut down the slight hint of retreat as she leveled her chin with the cave floor. "I'm a cop. I can protect myself."

"If you can connect the messages and stalking back to him, you'll have a stronger case, but you already know that." Hell, she advised the same protocol when dealing with domestic violence victims on the job. Which meant she wasn't telling him the whole truth. Closing the small distance between them, he admired the way she held her ground, the way she locked her back teeth and flexed the muscles along her jawline as though to prove how strong she was, how capable and driven. And damn, if that wasn't one of the sexiest things he'd ever seen. "As of right now, we have to assume no one is coming to save us, but I'm going to do everything in my power to get you to that hearing."

"How? We're literally trapped inside a mountain under several feet of snow, our pilot is missing and the plane is gone." Shea ran her hands along the cave wall, shadows consuming her from head to toe. "Unless you have a couple shovels in that bag of yours and something to keep us from freezing to death, we're on our own."

"Then that'll have to be enough." Vincent knelt beside the duffel of supplies Blackhawk Security operatives were required to carry, no matter the situation. Couple bottles of water, a day's worth of emergency food, first aid kit, change of clothes, space blanket, lighter, small bundle of kindling, anything portable they—or their clients— might need to survive the harsh temperatures of Alaska. He unpacked his SIG SAUER from the side pocket and checked the magazine in the flame of the lighter.

"Why are you helping me?" Her voice wavered as chills rocked through her. Shea attempted to warm herself by folding her arms across her chest, but her clothing had already been soaked through. The only thing that'd keep their bodies from sinking into hypothermia was a fire—and each other. "We're not exactly friends. We work together occasionally. Nothing more."

"Either we survive together, or we die alone. I don't know about you, but I prefer the former." He dug a flashlight from the bottom of the bag and let the lighter's flame die. Sweeping the beam over her, he studied the glistening wall at her back. Alaska was known for its gold and silver mines, but a handful of precious metals weren't going to keep them warm. "Night's already falling, so we're not getting out of here until morning. We need to search the cave and find a spot to build a fire. Only problem is ventilation. If we don't find the right spot and we light a fire, we'll—"

"Suffocate." She turned away from him, following the flashlight's beam up along the cavernous openings above them. "My brother was an Eagle Scout. I helped him with a lot of his merit badges."

"So what you're saying is you're going to be the one to make sure we don't die." Hauling the duffel over his shoulder, he ignored the pain spreading up his leg and treaded deeper into the cave. Blood trailed down the inseam of his pants and into his boots. Freezing temperatures had already worked deep into his muscles, slowing him down, but the addition of the sliver of shrapnel from the crash threatened to bring him to the edge. They had to find a place to camp and get the fire going. Only then would he worry about his leg. "Now I feel safe."

Her laugh curled around him from ahead, echoing off the bare walls of the cave, a deep, rich laugh he'd never heard from her before. What he wouldn't give to witness the smile accompanying the sound, but she'd already moved a few paces ahead of him, weapon drawn once again. Caves like this were perfect for wildlife native to these mountains. Bears, wildcats. They couldn't be too careful. "Don't get your hopes up. I wasn't paying that close attention."

A smile tugged at one corner of his mouth. Of all the people who could've stepped foot on that plane, the second passenger had to be Shea Ramsey. Intelligent, driven, beautiful. She'd pulled at something inside him the moment she was assigned to assist one of Blackhawk's past investigations, a need he hadn't thought about since waking up in the middle of the crime scene he was supposed to die in.

Darkness intensified his other senses as they felt their way deeper into the cave, his awareness of her—of the way her jeans brushed together at the apex of her thighs, of how her hair fell across her back—at an all-time high. A rush of cold air hit him square in the face, and he dragged the flashlight beam along the ceiling. There. A small opening about thirty feet up that hadn't been covered in snow. Big enough to provide ventilation for a fire. Studying the ground around them, he kicked loose rocks and dirt away from the area. "We can build a fire here."

Shea rubbed her hands together in an attempt to warm herself, but it wouldn't be enough. Not out here. "Shouldn't we be looking for a way out?"

"We're not going anywhere tonight." Vincent dropped to one knee, unpacking the lighter and small bundle of kindling from his bag. Within a minute, a fire snapped, crackled and popped.

They'd been exposed to the coldest temperatures Mother Nature had to offer, and the twigs wouldn't last all night. He straightened, tearing his jacket from his shoulders, then lifted his soaked T-shirt over his head. "Do you want to be the big spoon or the little spoon?"

HE COULDN'T BE SERIOUS. Of all the members of the Blackhawk Security team, Vincent Kalani ranked first on the people she fought to avoid in the field, with the firm's private investigator, Elliot Dunham, in a close second. Didn't matter that they'd crash-landed in the middle of the mountains and had to conserve body heat. She'd freeze to death before considering stripping out of her wet clothing in front of him. She attempted to control nervous energy in her gut, her chest still aching from where she'd been pinned against her seat in the plane. Vigilantes didn't follow the laws she'd sworn to uphold. And she didn't trust him. "I'd just as soon spoon a bear."

Heat drained from her neck and face as Vincent turned toward her. Intricate tattoos stretched across valleys and ridges of muscle all along his arms, up his sides and across his chest, and his question fled to the back of her mind. Her mouth dried as she studied him, studied the scars marring the designs along his shoulders when he laid his wet clothing on the ground to dry. So many of them. Curiosity urged her to close the distance between them, to run her fingers over the waves of puckered skin to see if they felt as soft as they looked. Did the scars stretch down his back, too?

"Considering where we are, that can probably be arranged. Although you might not live long enough to enjoy it. At least I don't bite. Unless you ask me nicely." His voice was gravelly. Vincent locked dark brown eyes on her, shadows dancing across his expression. Straightening to his full height, he suddenly seemed so much…bigger than he had before. He wiped his hands on his T-shirt as he approached with supple grace. "Got something you want to ask me, Officer Ramsey?"

She'd been staring. Taking a step back, she tried to gain control of her expression and the rush of emotions flooding through her. "I didn't realize you'd been injured."

"Yeah, well, there's a lot you don't know about me." He turned away from her, dark hair falling over powerful shoulder and back muscles. "Or my team."

She had to give him that.

"Can I…" She swiped her tongue between her lips. His heated gaze snapped to her mouth, and a rush of awareness chased back the tremors rocking through her. Her fingers tingled, but she wasn't sure if it was from the sensation returning to her hands or something more. Something that had nothing to do with hypothermia and everything to do with the man standing a few feet ahead of her. "Can I touch them?"

"What?" He lowered his hands to his sides, shock evident in the way he narrowed his eyes on her, in the way his voice dropped into dangerous territory.

Oh no.

"I'm sorry. I…" Shea blinked to clear her head, the spell broken. Her mouth parted. Had she really asked him if she could touch his scars? What the hell was wrong with her? "I didn't mean—"

"Nobody's ever asked me that before," he said. "Most people avoid them."

Most people? As in previous lovers? The fire crackled beside them. Her heart threatened to beat out of her chest as sympathy pushed through her. She'd understood the feeling of rejection all too well toward the end of her marriage, and the sudden urge to connect with Vincent reared its head. Or maybe she'd ignored her own needs for too long. She swallowed around the tightness in her throat. Nothing would happen between them. Not even if they were the last two people on earth. Swiping her suddenly damp palms on her jeans, she shook her head and stared into the fire. "I shouldn't have asked."

Vincent unzipped his duffel bag and dumped the contents onto the cave's floor. "We need to inventory our supplies and rest up."

Right. Because they were trapped inside a mountain with no tools to get them out, no rescue on the way and no communication to the outside world. She tugged her phone from her jacket pocket, chilled by the damp fabric. Still no bars, and the battery had already lost half its life with the dropping temperatures. Damn it. Her long curls slid over her shoulder as she settled on a large rock within the flames' glowing perimeter. Guessing from the size of the fire, it wouldn't last through the night, and she closed her eyes in defeat. Shea locked her back teeth against the truth. Without Vincent, she wasn't getting to New York. Hell, she wasn't even getting out of this cave. "We're going to have to cuddle, aren't we?"

"Only if you want to survive the night." He separated his supplies into piles, then handed her one of the clear plastic containers with a red lid from his pack. Food? "Look at it this way, at least I'm not a bear."

Not the kind that would put her in immediate danger, anyway. The container emitted a slight warmth through to her numb fingers. Out here, clean water wouldn't be a problem with the dozens of feet of white snow, but food? They'd be lucky to find an animal who hadn't gone down for the winter. Even then, the only weapons they had were their sidearms. Not overly effective against larger prey, and too many risks involved using them. They might miss, wasting their ammunition, or the sound could trigger another avalanche. But this… "You brought food with you on the plane?"

"My mom makes sure I don't go anywhere without a couple containers of her homemade meals. Makes me lunch every day." A wistful smile tugged at his mouth as he pried the lid from his own container. Using his fingers, he scooped up a bite of rice and tilted his head back as he dropped it into his mouth. "Blackhawk requires all of its operatives to carry supplies, but we don't know how long we're going to be out here. We'll need to ration out our food and collect some water in the morning."

Aromas of raw fish, mangoes, cucumber and soy sauce tickled the back of her throat, and her stomach growled in response. Poke. One of her favorites. Shea couldn't remember the last time she'd eaten. As soon as she'd gotten Wells's location from the same former partner at the NYPD whom she'd asked for Vincent's service record, she'd packed a couple days' worth of clothes and toiletries and jumped on the first flight out of Merrill Field. Vincent was right. They didn't know how long they were going to be stranded out here without help, and she wasn't stupid enough to turn away a filling meal when the opportunity presented itself.

She unsealed the container, crusted blood staining her knuckles from the crash, and shifted the fleshy muscles in the backs of her legs to get comfortable on the rock beneath her. Tears burned in her lower lash line at the offering, but she wouldn't let her weakness show. She'd survived the lowest point in her life by clawing her way out, fought to prove she could be the mother Wells deserved by seeing doctors, therapists, committing herself to the job. She wouldn't break in front of Blackhawk's operatives, least of all this one. But damn it, why wouldn't he fit inside the box she'd created for him at the back of her mind? Why couldn't he just be the lawbreaking investigator she'd made him out to be instead of a fellow survivor offering her half of his provisions? He had no reason to help her. "You don't have to share your supplies with me."

"Like I said, we survive together or we die alone." Dark eyes studied her as he withdrew a fresh long-sleeved shirt from his bag and threaded his arms through the sleeves, but Shea knew he wouldn't find anything in her expression. She'd mastered locking down her feelings months ago, learned from her mistakes. The minute she'd lost Wells to her ex-husband in the custody battle, she had nothing left inside, and old habits died hard. "I don't know about you, but I don't plan on dying out here."

Neither did she. Splitting the amount of food he'd given her in half, Shea ate as much as she dared and saved the rest for their next meal. There was nothing more for them to do tonight. Maybe in the morning, with the sun higher in the sky, they'd be able to navigate their way through the rest of the cave. Until then, they'd have to save their energy. Because this nightmare was far from over.

Vincent unpackaged a silver space blanket with his teeth, tearing through the plastic before smoothing out the fold lines. The material reflected the fire's brightest flames. "Put your jacket close to the fire so it can dry while we still have enough kindling. Do you have any other clothes in that bag?"

"A couple days' worth." But nothing that would hold up against temperatures hitting twenty below. Unlike him, she hadn't prepared for their plane to crash in the middle of nowhere. "Do you always carry around an entire arsenal of gear, or were you on your way to a survival expo?"

"No. It's part of my contract with Blackhawk."

His laugh echoed through the cave, deep, rumbling, warming her in places she'd forgotten existed. Could be she'd ignored her own needs for too long, or the fear of dying alone without ever seeing her son again had hiked her body's systems into overdrive. Whatever the case, she'd hold on to it as long as she could. To prove she could still feel something. Vincent maneuvered around the fire, space blanket in hand, before taking position on the ground with his back to the nearest wall. A defensive habit she recognized in soldiers and cops who'd been on the job for too long. "Every operator has to be prepared to protect and assist our clients, no matter the situation. Sometimes that includes plane crashes in the middle of the damn mountains."

"I guess that makes me lucky you were on that plane, too." He'd saved her life. And no matter how much it pained her to admit it, she'd never forget it. Shrugging out of her coat, she laid it flat at the base of the rock she'd taken up, her arms suddenly exposed to the frigid cold. She'd lived in Anchorage most of her life, her parents moving her and her twin brother to the last frontier when they were only toddlers after her father's career in engineering took a sharp dive. She knew how deadly the cold could be. Wrapping her arms around herself, she settled into the thin layer of dirt coating the cave floor in front of him, lying on her side to face the fire. Exhaustion, muscle soreness and his close proximity triggered tension down her back. Then increased as he shifted closer, but she couldn't ignore the heat he provided. "I still have my gun, Kalani. Don't think I won't use it if you get handsy."

Another deep laugh reverberated through him, fighting to break apart the knots down her back from behind. "Wouldn't dream of it, Officer Ramsey."

Chapter Three

She was asleep in his arms.

They'd survived the night despite losing their main source of heat, their bodies keeping each other warm. Her curls caught in his beard, and Vincent pulled his head back. His right arm had fallen asleep with the weight of her head on him, but he reveled in the feel of her body pressed against his. When had he wrapped his free arm around her waist? Sweat built at the base of his spine, but he didn't dare move. Not when the woman in his arms fit against him so perfectly, a woman who hadn't turned away from his scars in shock and disgust as so many others had.

They couldn't stay here. Someone out there had possibly brought their plane down, and there was a chance whoever had would scour these mountains to ensure they'd finished the job. Whether it was Shea's ex-husband as she believed or someone from his past, he had no idea. But he'd find out. The fact that his flight had taken a nosedive in the middle of the Chugach mountain range right after he'd had a break in the case couldn't be a co-incidence. Maybe, after everything she'd already been through, Shea Ramsey had simply been in the wrong place at the wrong time. Maybe his past had finally caught up with him. No way to con-firm unless they found the plane. And to do that, they had to get out of this damn cave.

"Please tell me it was all just a dream. I'm going to open my eyes, and none of this will be real." Her sleep-frogged voice caused the hairs on the back of his neck to stand on end, and it didn't take much to imagine waking to that voice any-where else but on the floor of a snowed-in cave. Dangerous territory. He had a job to do—a case to solve—and no matter how driven, pragmatic and sexy as hell she was, he couldn't afford to lose his focus. There were too many lives at risk. She lifted her head, untangling herself from the circle of his arms, and pinned beautiful jade-green eyes on him. Swiping her hair out of her face, she sat up, clothing mostly dry, and shoved away from him. "Ugh. No such luck."

"Good morning to you, too, Freckles." Cool air rushed over his exposed skin without her added body heat. Vincent straightened, locking back the groan working up his throat at the pain in his leg, and reached for the jacket he'd laid out the night before. Dressing, he stood, stretching the soreness out of his back as Shea grabbed the single roll of toilet paper from their pile of supplies and wandered farther into the cave, out of sight. He grabbed one of the food containers they'd rationed last night, downed a handful of rice and fish, and started packing. This early in the year sunlight only lasted six hours at most. They had to get moving if they were going to prove the plane had been sabotaged and try to contact rescue. Footsteps registered off to his left, and he nodded toward the food he'd saved for her. "Eat up. We don't have much time to find the plane."

"10-4." Shea finished off the container, handed it back to him, and shrugged into her coat and pack. Ready in less time than it took most of his team to prep for tactical support. For a woman who'd woken up with a piece of debris crushing her chest in the middle of the wilderness, she'd taken their situation better than he'd expected. No questions. No complaints. Impressive. Then again, Shea had been trained in all kinds of high-level circumstances just as he had with the NYPD. Hostage negotiation, standoffs with gunmen, dangerous pursuits, interrogations and more. Everything about her was impressive. But last night, he'd seen a different version of her from the cop he'd gotten to know over the past few months, the cop he'd gotten to admire for her sheer professionalism. She'd given him a glimpse beyond the emotionless mask she'd secured during their joint investigations, and, with her guard seemingly back in place, Vincent found himself wanting more.

"Have you ever patched a pair of jeans before?" He shifted his injured leg toward her, barely enough light coming through the opening above them to make it visible. The pain had dulled overnight, but blood was still oozing into his pant leg. If he didn't get the wound taken care of before they trekked through the snow, it'd become infected.

"What?" Those mesmerizing eyes of hers caught sight of blood. In an instant, she closed the distance between them, crouching in front of him. Down on one knee, she framed the wound in the side of his thigh with both hands, and every cell in his body sang with a rush of electricity. "How long were you planning on keeping that to yourself?"

"I need you to remove the shrapnel and stitch the wound, if you wouldn't mind," he said. "I'd do it myself, but it's at an odd angle. There's a needle, thread and some rubbing alcohol inside the first aid kit in the bag."

She pulled the kit from his duffel and located the medical supplies. Washing her hands with the alcohol, she handed the bottle to him to do the same to his leg. Stinging pain raced down his leg a split second before Shea came back into focus. Hesitation flared in her expression as she turned back to him, the box of sewing thread and needles in her hand. "Any color preference?"

"Black is fine." The breath rushed out of him as she tore the hole in his pants wider, her fingers icy against his skin. Metal on rock resounded through the cave as she tugged the piece of shrapnel from his muscle. In minutes, Shea had cleaned and stitched the wound and secured a fresh piece of gauze over the injury. Couldn't say she wasn't efficient. "Thanks."

"Any time." Cleaning her hands once again, she packed the supplies and handed him a roll of duct tape to patch the hole in his jeans. Out here, exposure would kill them faster than anything else, especially if the wind had picked up overnight. "Now let's get the hell out of here."

They moved farther into the cave, systematically following piercing rays of sunlight to find an opening big enough for them to escape. So far, nothing. A combination of cold humidity and staleness dived into his lungs as they moved, but not enough to choke out Shea's familiar scent, and he couldn't help but breathe a bit deeper. Columns of stalactites and stalagmites were closing in on both sides of the path ahead. They'd already spent too long trying to find an opening, but if they couldn't venture any farther, there was no way they were getting out of here before they starved.

"I think there's an opening up ahead." Her words vibrated through him with the help of the bare rock walls narrowing in around them, pushing him harder. The stitches in his leg stretched as Shea half jogged toward the largest pool of sunlight they'd come across so far. Her bright smile flashed wide as she turned back toward him, and his heart jerked in his chest. From the sight of her happy or from their discovery, he didn't know— didn't care. They'd found an escape.

Melting ice dripped onto his shoulders from above as they passed into the outside world, exposed skin tightening at the sudden change in temperature. Vincent pulled his T-shirt over his mouth and nose as his lungs ached from dropping temperatures. The plane had gone down on the north side of the peak, and this entrance to the cave sat on the west. They'd have to navigate to the other side in several feet of snow and treacherous heights to get to the crash site. Climbing and hiking had been one of his passions over the years, but it'd been a long time since he'd been in the mountains, and he sure as hell hadn't climbed in this much snow. They'd have to take this one step at a time. A gust of wind blew snowflakes in front of

them, whiting out his vision for a moment. Hell.
Without getting to the plane, they couldn't contact
his team or confirm his suspicions. They'd die out
here. Which meant they didn't have a choice. Not
if they wanted to survive. "I need you to take my
hand. Follow in my footsteps, got it? It's the only
way we're going to be able to do this."

"Okay." Nodding, she interlocked her fingers
with his, gripping him tight as he took the first
step. His boots disappeared into the sea of white,
but he hit solid ground. Slowly he led them alongside the peak, his back to the mountain, Shea close
on his heels. Each step brought them closer to the
curve of the rock. The wind threatened to unbal-
ance them, but right now, they had all the time in
the world. Nothing existed outside of the small
pocket of reality they'd created between the two of
them. Nothing but the next step. She'd expressed
her distrust with the Blackhawk Security team—
more than once—but in this moment, she was re-
lying on him to keep her alive, to get her back to
her son. He wouldn't fail her.

"Almost there!" The howling wind whipped
his words away. The sudden pain in his leg buckled his knee, and his foot slid beneath the snow.
Her short-lived scream echoed in his head as she
clenched his hand tighter. He righted himself before he slid down the mountain and pulled her in

close. Sweat built between their palms. His heart threatened to beat out of his chest as he reevaluated their plan. They were in this—100 percent—and they couldn't give up now. They followed the curve around the northwest corner of the mountain, and the wind immediately died. Crystalized puffs of air formed in front of his mouth as he took in the sun glittering off the tumble of snow that'd buried them beneath the rock. Without thought, he brought her into the circle of his arms as relief coursed through him. Neither of them would've survived the night without the other. He might've helped save her life during the avalanche, but without her, he wouldn't have made it this far.

Her body stiffened beneath his touch, and he instantly backed off. Right. They didn't know each other, not really, but it was the way her eyes narrowed on a single point over his shoulder that triggered his internal warning system. She nodded, his name on her lips barely a whisper over the wall of wind howling through the trees. "Vincent."

He turned to see what she'd locked onto.

The plane's hull had been cleared, leaving it bare to the elements.

"Is that…?" Disbelief tinted her voice as she fought to catch her breath and stumbled into him. "How is that possible?"

Vincent released her and unholstered his

weapon from beneath his coat. Thick trees impeded his view of the surrounding area, and his instincts prickled with awareness due to the fact that they were clearly out in the open. Vulnerable. "Because someone's already been here."

THEY WEREN'T ALONE.

"The pilot could've survived." Shea ducked deeper into her coat that wasn't nearly as thick as it should've been out here. She'd added a few more layers beneath, but the wind chill had dropped temperatures well below freezing. Her ears burned without anything to stop the cold from seeping in, the numbness in her toes and cheeks spreading. Her fingers tingled with pins and needles as Vincent released her hand, and she flexed them into the center of her palms inside her gloves. They'd made it back to the crash site, survived the night. Only they weren't the only ones. "He could still be out here. Maybe hurt."

There'd been so much blood on the windshield, she couldn't imagine their pilot would last long out here on his own, but there was a chance. If he was able to get to what was left of the plane's supplies, he could've staved off hypothermia for a little while longer. But then why not stay with the plane and wait for help?

Vincent shook his head as he circled around

the plane's remains, attention on the ground. He kept a wide perimeter as though studying a scene and was trying to keep evidence contamination to a minimum. Out here, though, it wouldn't be long until the winds and the fresh snow buried it all over again. "I count at least four sets of footprints here."

"A rescue team then." Shea didn't dare let the hope blossoming in her chest settle. No one from the tower had answered their Mayday call, and they would've heard a chopper or another plane searching the area by now. Wouldn't they?

"No one brings down a passenger plane without good reason. Wouldn't get as much attention as a commercial flight, and there's no guarantee anyone would see the crash or find us out here." He reached through the shattered front window into the cockpit and tugged something free, and her stomach wrenched. The handheld radio wire had been cleanly severed from the device. Not a rescue team. Which meant... "Whoever unburied the plane was looking for something. Or someone." His massive shoulders rolled beneath his coat, snow sticking to his dark beard. "Which means one of us, including our missing pilot, could be a target for the people who did this."

No. No, no, no, no. Shea stumbled back a few feet, snow working into the tops of her boots. This was crazy. The adrenaline from the crash had worn off and now her wild theory about Logan didn't make sense. Her ex wouldn't hire a team of men to ensure she never made it to New York. They hadn't ended their marriage on the best of terms, but to outright want her dead because she hadn't signed her parental rights away crossed a line. There was no way he'd do that to Wells. Despite the bitterness she'd held on to for the past few months for Logan leaving her, for moving Wells across the country, she had no doubt he loved their son. Her ex wouldn't risk losing the one thing that mattered to them both. "Logan wouldn't do this. He doesn't have the funds to hire anyone to sabotage a plane or a motive to want me dead. I'm not trying to take Wells from him. I just want to see my son."

Vincent dropped his duffel into the snow and ducked into the side door of the plane, where one of the wings had been torn clean off by the rocks during their descent. "I've known people to kill for a lot less."

Unfortunately, so had she. More recently, while working a case with Blackhawk's private investigator, Elliot Dunham, and a woman Shea believed to be a murderer. In the end, the real killer had left a trail of bodies for fear he'd lose everything if news he carried the warrior gene found in his genetic makeup went public. She'd been the arresting officer on that case, forced to work beside Vincent Kalani at the chief's orders, to prove Elliot's client had been framed. So many lives taken for the sake of holding on to a reputation.

It hadn't been her and Vincent's first case together, but she'd done everything in her power since then to ensure it'd be their last. The way her breathing changed when he studied her, the way her heart rate picked up pace when he neared, even how every muscle down her spine seemed to relax when she caught his clean, masculine scent... Working cases with him had helped her break through the fog that'd cut her off from her family, friends and coworkers, made her feel things she hadn't felt since before giving birth to her son. But it wasn't enough to convince her he and his team were above the law.

A hunk of metal landed beside her boot, pulling her back into the present. Her ears rang. Terrifying memories seared across her brain as Vincent tossed more debris into the snow, and she focused on pushing one foot in front of the other to aid in whatever search he was navigating. Didn't matter they'd been stranded together or that they'd be partnered together on future cases between the department and Blackhawk. She wouldn't give in to the desirable impulses carving at the hollowness inside. Not with him. "What are you looking for?"

"The black box is gone." Vincent pulled free of the hull and dusted snow and dirt from his jacket before turning to her. Solid exhales formed in front of his mouth as he ran a hand down his beard. He slammed his fist into the side of the plane, and she flinched as the sound bounced off the peaks around them. "All the emergency supplies are missing, too. Probably sucked out the back with the rest of the cargo when the tail ripped off." His shoulders heaved with his overexaggerated breathing before he locked dark brown eyes on her. "What we have won't last more than a day, two at most."

"Then we need to try to get out of here on foot. West." Her gaze slid to the black duffel bag at his feet, and she threaded her arms through her pack, bringing it around to her front. Shea dropped to her knees and consolidated everything into the one bag. Easier to carry than the duffel but would leave one person without supplies if they were separated. In less than a minute, she slung it back into place, fingers gripped around the straps, and faced him. They could switch off carrying the supplies to conserve energy and camp for the night when it got dark. Leaving the plane was a risk. What if someone in the tower had heard their distress call? What if the footprints did actually belong to a rescue team? What if they were making a mistake?

They were lost someone where in the middle of the Chugach Mountain range, with mountains surrounding them in every direction. Any attempt to head out of here on foot increased their chances of hypothermia, frostbite, starvation, getting lost, any number of possibilities that could end with their deaths. But Shea had to get to her son. And she wasn't going to let anything—anyone—else stand in her way. "The only way we're getting out of here is if we work together."

One step. Two. Vincent closed the distance between them, and she swallowed the urge to back away. To prove he didn't affect her. He brought his gloved hand up, setting his fingers at the back of her neck. Ice clung to where his gloves touched her exposed skin, but in that moment, she could only focus on the pressure building behind her sternum. "And here I thought you've been avoiding having to work with me."

She could still smell him on her. A mixture of something spicy and wild. Every time she moved, she resurrected the scent, but it was even more powerful now that he'd breached her personal space. An overwhelming sense of calm spread down her back and across her shoulders. Shea opened her mouth, not really sure how to respond—

A gunshot exploded from above.

The reaction was automatic. Her vision blurred as she slammed into him, and they fell into more than three feet of snow together. His hands wrapped around her arms to pull her off him as reality set in. They were out in the open. Vincent brought his head up, scanning the surrounding area a split second before he tugged her to her feet. Adrenaline surged through her as they headed for the closest patch of trees, his injury making him limp, her lungs on fire. The pack slowed her down, but she wouldn't ditch it with the possibility they'd have to keep running.

She skimmed her gloves over rough bark and doubled over to catch her breath. Searching up through the branches of the large pine, Shea watched for movement, listened for another shot—anything—that would give them an idea of what they were up against. She swiped her hand across her runny nose. "These mountains carry sound for miles."

"The shot sounded like it came from close by." His weapon was in his hand. His lighthearted expression she'd gotten used to since they'd crashed faded into a stone-cold wall of unreadability, as though he'd tear any threat apart with his bare hands. Vincent Kalani had served New York City as one of the best forensic investigators in the country, but in that moment, he'd become one of

Blackhawk's vigilantes. Powerful. Dark. Dangerous. "But that doesn't make me feel any better,
either."

"We need to go." They couldn't stay here. No
telling if the team who'd unburied the plane had
fired that shot or if they were here to help at all.
Whatever the case, Shea wasn't interested in finding out.

A twig snapped from behind, and she spun,
unholstering her weapon in the same move. She
took aim as Vincent maneuvered in front of her,
as though he intended to use himself as a shield to
protect her. Her breath shuddered through her, the
cold stiffening her trigger finger as they studied
the shadows in the thick line of pines. Branches
dipped and swayed, and the tension Vincent had
chased back a moment ago climbed into her shoulders once again.

A man stumbled from the tree line, and she
tightened her grip on her weapon. Black slacks,
graying hair, white button-down shirt. Blood
spread from the injury in the center of his chest
and from a deep laceration on his head. Locking
his gaze on Shea, the man collapsed to his knees
and reached for her as he fell forward.

She lunged, catching their missing pilot before
he hit the snow. Her gun fell from her hand as
she laid his head back and studied the fresh bul-

let wound in his chest. She tugged her glove free with her teeth and set her fingers at the base of his neck. The breath rushed out of her. She looked up at Vincent, at a loss for words. It was too late. "He's dead."

Chapter Four

Their pilot was dead, they didn't have any way to contact the Blackhawk Security team, and there was at least one gunman closing in. He and Shea had to get the hell out of here.

They trudged through knee-deep snow as fast as they could between the trees, but the downward angle of the mountain threatened to trip them up with every step. His boot slid against hardened ice beneath the powder, but Shea kept him from rolling down the hill, one hand wrapped around his arm and the other around the tree closest to them. They'd had to leave the pilot where he fell. No time for a proper burial. Not with a killer possibly on their trail. He'd had basic medical training on the job, but it'd been too late. Someone out here had sabotaged their plane, cut their chances of communicating with the outside world, and already killed a man. Hell, he didn't even catch their pilot's name. The longer they stayed in one spot out here without moving, the higher the chance the cold would seep into them. Hypothermia was real. And it was deadly.

"Are we going to talk about what happened back there or pretend someone didn't just kill our pilot?" Her voice cut through the deafening silence around them. "At the crash site you said one of us might be the target of whoever took down the plane." The mountain blocked most of the wind, but an attractive red coloring spread over the freckles speckling her cheeks all the same. Her shallow breathing made her words breathy. "Why was that your first theory? Why not a terrorist attack or simple engine failure?"

"Our focus needs to be on surviving right now. Not theories." Vincent slowed his pace to give her a chance to catch her breath and take some weight off his injured leg. Scooping a handful of fresh snow into his mouth, he cleared the stickiness building under his tongue. A headache pulsed above his eyebrow where he'd swiped dried blood away. Must've gotten hit by something during the crash. Although he couldn't remember what it was. There were any number of reasons someone would've wanted to take down their plane. Any number of reasons they could be targets. In reality, too many to count. But none of them mattered out here. They'd left the safety of the cave out of necessity, but they wouldn't last long once night fell. They had to keep moving. He continued down the incline, but the lack of her familiar breathing said Shea hadn't followed.

"What aren't you telling me?" she asked.

Vincent turned back toward her, gravity pulling at one side. Pressure built from her intense questioning gaze, as though she were trying to read his mind to get the answers she deserved, and damn, he found himself powerless to the fire in her eyes in that moment. Powerless to her. "There's a chance this has to do something with the last case I was working for the NYPD."

She kicked up loose powder as she closed in, those mesmerizing green eyes still locked on him. "What case?"

Sense returned in small increments. He hadn't told anyone—not even his team—what'd happened that night. For good reason. The more people he got involved, the higher the risk to their lives. Then again, maybe he'd already sentenced Shea to death by getting on that plane.

"Doesn't matter." He stared out over the expanse of trees, rock and snow—miles of it—to escape the sickening clench in his gut every time those memories rushed to the surface. Vincent had fled to Anchorage and joined Blackhawk a year ago for one reason: to move on and to forget. Only now, with the discovery of a partial fingerprint from Internal Affairs Bureau Officer Ashton Walter's death scene, he couldn't hide from the truth any longer. Someone had killed two members of his forensic unit the day of the fire in an attempt to cover up the evidence left behind, but he'd survived. Now he was going to find out why. In any other circumstance, he would've had a lead on who'd tampered with the plane by now and possibly been able to connect the dots, but out here, with nothing but a day's worth of food, a first aid kit and a handgun, he was useless. "Unless we find shelter for the night, none of this is going to matter."

Shea moved into him, never breaking eye contact, so close he could count the freckles across the bridge of her nose. A bruise marred perfectly light olive skin across her left cheek, one he hadn't seen before now, as she drew her eyebrows inward. It was a small price compared to what could've happened when they'd crashed but still twisted his insides. If the people he'd suspected of killing that IAB officer had found him, Shea would be nothing but collateral damage to them. His fingers tingled with the urge to trace the dark outline of the bruise. Or was it frostbite finally settling in? She set her hand over his coat, directly over his heart, and his body temperature spiked. "Whatever you're hiding, it might've already tried to kill us." Her hand fell to her side, and he went cold as she pushed past him. "Just remember that in case we don't make it through the night."

He spun after her. "Shea, I—"

Bark splintered off the tree he was holding on to with a crack as loud as thunder, and Vincent fell forward. Her eyes widened a split second before he collided with her, then they were both falling. The gunman had caught up with them. Their surroundings blurred as they rolled down the incline, each clinging to the other. Momentum and gravity ripped her from his hands. Ice worked beneath his coat as he rolled, and all he could do was wait for the ride to end. Pain cracked down his spinal column what felt like hours later as he slammed into a large boulder. His head snapped back into rock, his ears ringing, but he forced himself to push to his feet. Couldn't stop. His vision wavered as Vincent stumbled forward. "Shea."

Where was she? Had she been hit?

The world righted itself, shouts echoing off the cliffs around them. He reached into his coat for his weapon but found only an empty shoulder holster. Damn it. He must've lost the gun when he'd rolled down the mountain. He'd tumbled at least one hundred feet. It could be anywhere. Snow clung to his hair and beard, and he shook his head to clear the haze holding tight. His heart threatened to beat out of his chest. "Shea!"

"I'm here. I'm okay." Movement caught his attention through the thick branches of a tree a few yards to his left seconds before her five-foot-three frame filled his vision. Relief swept through him at the sight of her, drawing him closer. Shooting her hands to his arms, Shea leaned on him, hiking his blood pressure higher, but he didn't have more than a few seconds to revel in the sensation. Her attention shot up the hill as shouts echoed down, and she sank a bit deeper on her back foot. She unholstered her weapon, fixing her index finger over the trigger through her gloves. Snow fell from the backpack of supplies and the ends of her hair as they took cover. "They're coming."

Determination and something he couldn't quite put his finger on pulled her shoulders back as she took aim. She was prepared to fight, but she couldn't hide the fear in her eyes.

"Listen to me. I need you to run. Don't look back. Don't wait for me." He'd hold them off. At least until she found cover. Crouching, Vincent scanned the trees, senses on alert. They didn't have much time before the shooter or shooters caught up with them. "I'll distract them as long as I can."

"From the sound of those voices, we're outnumbered and outgunned." Shea widened her stance

as the shouts grew closer. Brilliant emerald-green
eyes narrowed on him, and his breathing slowed,
as though his body had been specifically tuned to
hers over the past twelve hours. "I'm not leaving
you to face them by yourself. Survive together or
die alone, remember? We're going to figure this
out, but right now, we need to live until we can
get that chance."

A bullet ripped past them, and Vincent automatically shielded himself behind the closest tree.
They were pinned down. Any movement on their
part would expose them to the next shot. They
needed a distraction. These trees were thick, and
the team on the other side of those guns had to be
tactically trained. No way he and Shea could take
them out with only the sixteen rounds from her
weapon. "Toss me the pack."

She switched her weapon to her other hand before throwing their supplies at his feet. Another
shot tore through the bark mere inches from his
shoulder, and he dropped to the snow as Shea returned fire. Once. Twice. "I've got fourteen rounds
left."

The shots reverberated through him and off
the rocks surrounding them. He wrapped his grip
around the flare gun he'd taken from the small
case beneath one of the plane's seats. One shot.
That was all he needed. Arching around the tree,

he homed in on the dark clothing set against white snow about thirty feet above then took aim at the brush the bastard was using for cover and pulled the trigger.

The flare hit the dried tinder, catching it on fire within seconds. Black smoke billowed between them and the gunmen. The flame wasn't designed to last long. They had to move. "There's our chance, Freckles. Go!"

Shea took off, Vincent close on her heels, down the mountain. Muscles burned in his legs, the stitches in his thigh protesting every time he pulled his boot free from the powder, but he wouldn't slow down. Not until he got her the hell out of this mess. Another round of gunfire exploded from behind but never found its target. He pushed himself harder, careful to keep Shea in front of him as they sped down the incline in an effort to protect her from the next bullet.

The distraction had done its job, giving them enough time to put distance between them and the tactical team, but it wasn't permanent. Whoever'd sent those gunmen wanted something—or someone—and if they were anything like him and his team, they wouldn't stop until they got it.

SHE COULDN'T TAKE another step.

They'd been wandering through the wilderness, running off pure adrenaline, but Shea had nothing left to give. Her feet and hands had gone numb more than an hour ago, her lungs burning with every inhale. Ice crusted to her hair and eyelashes. One more step. That was all she had to focus on, but she couldn't do it. She leveraged her arm against the nearest tree for support. They were still miles away from civilization, with no idea where they—

She saw the glimpse of dark blue in a land of white, brown and green. Straight ahead, topped with inches of snow, surrounded by a clearing of pines. But... She didn't dare breathe. Was it real, or had hypothermia already set in? Was this her body's final attempt to survive by giving her false hope? Her mouth barely moved to form his name, the muscles in her jaw aching from the cold. "Vincent?"

"I see it," he said, and everything inside her released. "Looks like a ranger station."

A sob built in her throat. She collapsed into the powder as relief coursed through her, but Vincent was there, pulling her upright. Before she had a chance to protest, he swept her over his shoulder in a firefighter's hold. She couldn't imagine the amount of pain he must've been in with her added weight, admired him for making it this far with his injury, but he held her tight. His steps were strong, evenly paced, as he hiked over uneven rocky terrain leading to the ranger station.

"I've got you." His words vibrated down his back and into her chest, and she believed him. Just as she'd believed he would do everything possible to give her a chance to get to safety when the bullets had started flying, even at the cost of his own life. But she hadn't been able to leave him. Not when she'd taken an oath to protect and serve. Not when… Not when he'd gone out of his way to save her life after the crash. To keep her warm when their fire had gone out. To share his supplies when they both knew there was only enough food for one of them.

She had no reason to trust him, other than neither of them would make it out of here on their own, but the bitterness she'd clung to on the plane seemed stupid now. The edges of her vision darkened as he lowered her feet to the ground, but she failed to keep her balance and fell back.

But still, he was there. Even with his dark Hawaiian complexion, color had drained from his face, a thin layer of snow and ice clinging to his beard and exposed skin, but he hadn't complained once. Hadn't let her give up. Vincent tore his glove from one hand, the other centered on her lower back as he helped her sit. When had he gotten her inside? "Hang on, Freckles. Stay here while I try to get the heat going."

He disappeared deeper into the station, her gun in his hand.

Shea gave in to gravity, falling back on a single twin mattress shoved into the corner of the main room in the station. The National Park Service had cabins like this all over the mountains. They were used as shelters for backcountry hikers who hadn't been able to escape bad weather or for support for rangers circulating through the area for their shifts. Which meant they'd hiked into a national park. They weren't lost anymore. Seconds slipped by in silence. Minutes? She had to get up. Had to find Vincent and make sure he hadn't succumbed to hypothermia. Because without him, she wasn't going to ever see her son again.

Stinging needles exploded through her hands, and Shea forced her eyes open. Haloed by a warm, orangish glow from behind, Vincent centered in her vision. He rubbed her hands between his big, calloused palms. He'd pulled her boots and jacket free, layering her in a thick quilt she hadn't realized kept the tremors in her body at bay until now. She must've fallen asleep. Or passed out. She wasn't sure which she preferred, but the truth was, she knew she was lucky to be alive. "You saved my life again, didn't you?"

"We saved each other." He massaged heat and pressure into her hands, then her wrists and arms, a known technique for combating hypothermia to get the circulation in her body going again, but it was more than that. There were no visible signs of frostbite on her fingertips and toes, yet he hadn't stopped touching her. Dark brown eyes studied her from head to toe, the sensation so raw it felt as real as physical touch. Or was that the lingering effects of the cold-induced delirium? "I'd have a bullet in my back if it weren't for you tackling me like an NFL linebacker."

A small laugh bubbled past her lips. The past few hours of memories played back as he continued rubbing small circles into her arms, and the warmth he'd generated drained. Them finding the plane unburied, the pilot stumbling from the trees with a fresh bullet wound in his chest, the destroyed radio. It all fit with Vincent's theory. Someone had sabotaged the plane, then hired a team to ensure no one had survived the crash. But who? Who would want either of them dead? "Why is someone trying to kill us, Vincent? What happened on your last case?"

His strokes slowed, then he pulled away altogether, and her stomach jerked in protest. Running one hand through his hair, he leaned back in his chair. "My forensic unit was called to the scene of an officer-involved shooting back when I worked for the NYPD. An Internal Affairs investigator named Ashton Walter. He'd been killed in the warehouse district, but the medical examinor couldn't give us anything solid to identify a suspect, even with small amount of evidence my team collected—or wouldn't. The victim had been looking into a handful of unsolved homicide cases I brought to his attention after my commanding officer shot down my suspicion the killer had to have been familiar with crime scene procedure and forensics. According to her, Walter wasn't supposed to have been in that area and had most likely gotten involved in something he shouldn't have, but nothing I recovered from the scene supported that theory."

"You think he was killed because he was looking into your unsolved cases?" Her heart jerked in her chest. That amount of guilt could crush a person from the inside, even someone as insightful, intelligent and innovative as Vincent.

"Officer Walter was a good guy, good investigator. He had a wife and a kid on the way at the time. Brass couldn't prove their corruption theory, and Homicide was instructed to close the case." A disbelieving laugh rumbled through him. Vincent crossed his arms over his heavily muscled chest, gaze distant as though he wasn't really seeing her in front of him. Shadows danced across his expression from the single lantern he must've lit while she'd been unconscious, hiding his expression, but she caught the soberness in his words. "So I convinced a couple techs from my team to take another look at the scene on our own. I just…" His thick brows furrowed over the bridge of his nose, those dark eyes centered on her, and the crash, the gunmen, everything disappeared for the briefest of moments. "I couldn't let it go. I was trained to follow the evidence, but the place had been wiped clean before we'd gotten there. There was no evidence to follow, and less than two minutes after we arrived on scene someone knocked me unconscious. Next thing I knew, the entire place and everything in it was on fire. Including me."

Her breath shuddered out of her, and Shea wanted nothing more than to reach out to him, but any kind of sympathy from her paled in comparison to what he'd already been through. "That's how you got your scars."

"I got out." He nodded, pressing his shoulders into the back of the chair. "But the other two members of my team didn't."

"I didn't realize…" What? That he wasn't the only one with a guilty past? That the Blackhawk Security operative she'd built in her mind over the past year wasn't the man sitting in front of her?

Swallowing around the tightness in her throat, she pushed to sit up and swung her legs over the edge of the bed. In her next breath, she leaned into him, wrapping her arms around his neck, and held him. She didn't know what else to do, what else to say. The feel of him against her chased back the final tendrils of ice in her bones. Ducking her forehead into the tendon between his neck and shoulder, she breathed his earthy, masculine scent deeper. Until she couldn't take one more single sip of air. "I'm sorry."

The air around them shifted as Vincent threaded his arms to her lower back, holding her against him, and she gave in to him at that moment. Didn't matter she'd promised herself to keep her distance, not to get attached to the man she was so determined to hate. They'd survived a plane crash together, outrun an avalanche and fought off a team of gunmen after someone had killed their pilot in cold blood. She needed this. Right now, she needed to feel something.

Shea turned her head upward, planting a small kiss against his jawline, and pleasure unlike anything she'd ever felt before immediately shot through her. She and Logan had done what all married couples were supposed to do. They'd conceived Wells together, but this... This was different. She slid her mouth along the veins in Vincent's neck, smiled as his breathing shallowed, and a tremor shook his mountainous shoulders. *This* was unfiltered physical want. What *she* wanted. Something she hadn't let herself give in to for so long.

She'd traded her own path for the things others expected from her most of her life. She'd joined the Anchorage PD after her twin brother had been killed in the line of duty to carry on the family blue blood. She'd married the boy next door at her mother's insistence that she move on after the funeral. She'd gotten pregnant after Logan had convinced her a baby would fix their problems. She'd given everything to live up to her friends' and family's expectations and had been the only one left with the consequences afterward.

Vincent's beard bristled against her oversensitized skin as she framed his face with her opposite hand. Logic battled desire. They were practical strangers, believed in wholly different ideals. Not to mention someone had sent a team of gunmen to hunt them down, but, in this moment, none of that mattered. It was only the two of them here.

Now it was her turn to be happy.

Chapter Five

"Shea..." Damn, she felt good, her lips pressed against his throat. Vincent dug his fingers into lean muscle along her rib cage. He'd imagined this moment so many times before, to the point he hadn't been able to tell the difference between reality and his fantasies as he'd wrapped his arms around her back in the cave. The moment was real—she was real—but this couldn't happen between them. "We can't."

She swiped the tips of her fingers against his lips, a combination of salt and her sweetness flooding his system. An extra surge of desire exploded as she maneuvered off the bed and straddled powerful thighs on either side of him. Her frame fit against him perfectly as she explored the sensitive spot under his ear, and he couldn't hold back the quake of desire rocketing through him. "Don't say anything."

"This is just the stress of the situation." He'd

said the words to convince himself more than any-thing else. They'd been through a lot over the past eighteen hours. The crash, nearly getting buried in the avalanche, surviving the night with only each other's body heat. Now the hit team tracking them through the wilderness. He couldn't blame her for giving in to the adrenaline. Hell, right now that seemed like the best damn idea to ignore re-ality, but he wouldn't take advantage of it. She'd made her feelings about him—about the way he worked—abundantly clear since they'd investi-gated their first case together. Even in the face of death, she didn't trust him. Gripping her arms, Vincent slowly settled her back onto the edge of the mattress. "We don't want to do anything we'll both regret."

When this happened between them—and it would—it wasn't going to be because of some chemical reaction brought on by fear or despera-tion. She'd want him as much as he'd wanted her these past few months, and there'd be no claiming it was a mistake in the morning.

Shea blinked at him, her lips parted, almost as though she didn't know what'd come over her. "You're right. I think I got caught up in the mo-ment. That won't happen again." Brushing her curls back with one hand, she leveraged one hand against her knee, her attention on the lantern he'd lit. A quick laugh burst past the seam of her lips as she slid her gaze to him without turning to face him. "Are you going to be completely awkward around me now?"

He couldn't help but smile. The woman owned up to her impulse and tried to get him to laugh about it in the process. Damn that only made him want her more. If it weren't for the fact that their lives were at risk, Vincent wouldn't have stopped her. "Totally."

"Great. Glad we're in agreement on something." Pushing off the bed, she crossed the main room of the station. The same fingertips she'd brushed against his mouth slid across the desk against one wall, then the stone fireplace as she moved deeper into the shadows the lantern's light couldn't reach. All too easily, he imagined that fireplace alight, the flames reflected in her gaze as she whispered his name in pleasure. "These stations usually only have a minimal food and water supply, no firearms or ammunition, and too many sight lines for the two of us to cover. With all these windows, we're easy targets to whoever's tracking us, and we can't just hunker down until we contact your team. So what's our next move?"

His thoughts exactly, which only left them with one option. "We wait." Vincent hauled himself to his feet, his steps thundering across the old wooden floor as he closed the distance between them. "Let them come to us."

"You want to set a trap," she said.

It was the only way to keep her safe, to ensure the coming fight didn't affect her chances of getting her son back. "I recovered what I thought was a partial fingerprint before I escaped the fire that night. It'd been melted into the handle of a gasoline can nearby. I ran it in every database I could get access to after I relocated to Anchorage with no matches, but now I don't think it was a partial at all." Vincent scrubbed his hand down his beard, tugging on the hair toward the end. "I think whoever set that fire, whoever wanted to destroy all the evidence of that IAB officer's murder, I think the killer burned him or herself in the process bad enough to erase half of their print. I want to know who."

"You think the person who killed your vic is the one who hired the team waiting out there." Shea parted the curtains he'd drawn over the windows to lower the shooter's visibility, just enough for her to scan the area. Apparently satisfied, she turned back toward him. "Why send them now? You said you recovered that print a year ago, that you've been running searches in the databases all that time."

He'd been wondering about that, too, but Vincent already knew the answer. He'd known it the minute the plane's engine had failed. Maybe even before that, but the work he and his team did for Blackhawk brought all kinds of threats. Being followed came with the territory. Their clients came to them for one reason: protection. Stood to reason the operatives hired to do the protecting would be put at risk in the process. Hell, he'd be surprised if he wasn't being followed on a daily basis. "Because I got on a plane to New York."

"Someone was watching you." Shea clasped her hands over the back of the desk chair, dropping her head down as she widened her stance. "They were waiting to see if you'd keep the investigation going on your own, and when you got on the plane, they wanted to make sure you wouldn't have the chance." She straightened, hands on her hips. "No matter who else was on board."

A sickening swirl of nausea churned in his gut. "Shea, I never meant for you to get involved. If I'd known—"

"I am on the brink of losing my son because of you. The custody hearing is in two days, and I'm not going to be there to fight for him. Everything I've done over the past year to prove I can be the mother he deserves was for nothing." Controlled rage raised the veins in her arms, the tendons between her neck and shoulders stark in the dim light. She pointed one long finger toward the floor. Disgust and fire contorted her expression before she turned away from him, shadows darkening the bruise on her face. Unshed tears reflected the small flame from the lantern. Facing him again, Shea stepped into him, every bit the officer he'd encountered during their investigations. "You could've gone to the police. You could've involved your former CO and gotten the case reopened, but instead of following the rules like everyone else, you put other people's lives in danger. Our pilot is dead out there with a gunshot in his chest because you and your team think you're above the law, that you're better than everyone else." She collected her gun and backpack from the desk where he'd set them earlier and headed toward the short hallway separating the front of the station from the rooms in the back. "I hope you can live with that when this is over."

Vincent only stared after her, curling his fingers into his palms. Because she was right. He could keep telling himself he'd pursued this investigation on his own to protect the people around him, but he knew the truth. Just as she did. It'd been his personal need for justice that'd kept him from reaching out to his old commanding officer, from trusting anyone else but himself with the evidence he'd recovered. He wanted to be the one to punish whoever'd killed his teammates that night, who'd tried to kill him. Just like the vigilante she'd accused him of being. But no matter how many times he'd convinced himself otherwise, he wasn't alone in this. Shea had been dragged into this nightmare the moment she'd stepped on that damn plane.

He traced her steps down the hall, following the sounds of rustling in one of the back rooms, then stilled as he studied her from the doorway of the communications-room-slash-pantry. Dark, curly hair fell in waves down her back as she riffled through the boxed food on the single shelf, and the blood drained from his upper body. No apology could possibly make up for what he'd done, especially if missing the custody hearing kept her from her son permanently, but he'd sure as hell try. "Shea—"

"We should use the station's radio to try to put the call out to Anchorage PD." Lean muscle flexed along her arms as she scooped extra food and supplies into the backpack, the gun at the hollow in her back. She wouldn't look at him, wouldn't even turn in his direction, her anger a physical presence between them. "Assuming the tactical team out there is listening, they'll know exactly where to find us. Then we can put this whole thing behind us and go our separate ways. Move on with our lives."

Move on. She'd already gone out of her way to avoid working with him on joint investigations with Blackhawk Security these past few months. How much more distance did she intend to wedge between them? Vincent stepped into the room, gripped her arms and compelled her to look up at him. Her muscles stiffened beneath his hands in warning. Or was that her body's natural defense kicking in? Either way, Shea Ramsey obviously saw him as a threat, which was the last thing he wanted. He released his hold on her. Gave her the space she needed. "You were right. I could've involved the police or my team, but I wanted to be the one to bring down the bastard who tried to kill me that night." Hearing the words coming from his own mouth made them real, confirmed what he'd felt deep inside since escaping to Anchorage over a year ago. The NYPD didn't want him anymore, but that wouldn't stop him from getting justice the victims of those unsolved cases deserved. That he deserved. "Say what you want about Blackhawk and the work we do, but my team and me? We will do whatever it takes to get the job done, even when that means we have to break a few rules along the way. We fight for our clients. No matter the cost." Vincent swiped his knuckles alongside her jaw, smooth skin catching against the rough patches on the back of his hand, and her green eyes widened slightly. "Because when it comes to protecting the people we care about, there are no rules."

He crushed his mouth to hers.

SHE COULDN'T THINK. Couldn't breathe. Couldn't believe she was kissing him back.

His mouth on hers seared her skin, through muscle and into bone, and Shea couldn't force herself to turn away. She'd dreamed of this moment so many times. Late at night, alone in that empty house after she'd gotten home from working a long shift. Most of the calls she and her partner responded to on the job included robbery or violent crime, but the ones when she'd been paired with Blackhawk Security—with Vincent—brought her back from the darkness piece by piece.

The cases they'd worked together challenged her, tested her mental and physical endurance, gave her something new to focus on, even if she didn't agree with the firm's methods. Working investigations with him had given her a strength she'd forgotten she'd had, to the point she'd finally asked for professional help from her obstetrician then the department's counselor a few months ago. Vincent had unknowingly given her hope, a reason to keep going when the postpartum depression had convinced her she couldn't help anyone. Not even herself.

He maneuvered her backward until the back of her thighs hit the small desk with the radio equipment with a jolt, not breaking the kiss once. His tongue penetrated the seam of her mouth and the world exploded around her. He skimmed his hands around her lower back, wrapping her in the protective circle of his arms. That single touch awakened a sense of safety, of warmth, she'd forgotten existed since her ex had served her with custody papers, and she never wanted it to end. The small gasp of satisfaction at the back of her throat was followed by a laugh, and she set her hand against his chest to push away.

Her skin felt too tight, the thud of her heart too fast in her chest. Damn, the man could kiss, but he was right. This was nothing more than a pressure release in a stress-induced situation. A biological reaction her body needed to get back that sense of adrenaline. Hardened muscle formed ridges and valleys under her fingertips.

Because when it comes to protecting the people we care about, there are no rules.

Had he meant her? Shea traced a piece of loose thread in his shirt, a distraction from the wave of desire washing over her from the inside. "Why did you request me as your partner on the joint investigations between the department and Blackhawk?"

After seeing for herself how Vincent worked—

how many laws he and his team ignored in their search for justice—she'd asked her captain to remove her as one of the investigators from the small partnership their respective organizations had formed. Only to learn the truth in the process: Vincent had specifically asked to work with her on the threat that he'd shut down the task force if her captain partnered him with anyone else.

Seconds ticked by. A minute? Shea forced herself to raise her gaze to his, the beat of his heart spiking under her palm, and she was immediately captivated by the inferno in his eyes. The walls closed in. There was a team of killers outside those walls, but right in that moment, he made her feel as though they were the only two people in the world.

"I've never been able to ignore a good puzzle. You're driven but adaptable. You stick to your core values and uphold the law, even at your own personal risk, but you'll pull your weapon on me for the chance to get your son back. I think you truly care about the people you serve and protect in this city, but you won't align yourself with Blackhawk because you don't agree with our methods when we're trying to do the same thing." His hands slid along her lower back, fighting back the cold creeping in as the sun went down. The battle invoked a shiver she couldn't repress across her shoulders, and she hated the fact that her body reacted to it, to him. "You're out to prove yourself, and that makes you a good cop, one I'm proud to have at my side. But to tell you the truth, none of that matters to me. Not really."

"It doesn't?" she asked.

"No." Vincent tangled his fingers through the hair at the nape of her neck; his large palm settled under her ear. "I requested you because not only are you a top-notch pro, but also one look from you makes me forget the nightmare I live with every day since waking up in the middle of that fire." He stared down at her, his eyes glittering in the dim light of the lantern she'd brought in here with her, and her breath caught. "The only thing I can't figure out is what you're hiding."

The hairs on the back of her neck stood on end, and Shea dropped her hands away from his chest. Impossible. There was no way he could see through her defenses that easily. Not with all the hard work she'd put into keeping up appearances. Her partner hadn't known she and Logan had divorced until she'd told him a few months ago. Had Vincent seen more? "What makes you think I'm hiding something?"

"I'm good at my job." Vincent stepped back, taking his body heat with him, and the cold started creeping in again. Physical or mental, she had no idea, didn't want to know. "I don't need to know your secrets, Shea. I need you to trust me. I'll do everything I can to get us out of this alive, and I'm not going to give up until I do. I'll get you to your son."

She'd spent the past year in a fog, unable to focus, so mad at everyone and everything around her because her mind hadn't been able to handle the transition to motherhood. She'd isolated herself from her friends, her family, from the things that'd once made her happy. She'd lost everything that mattered to her in the span of a few months. First, her husband when he couldn't understand what was happening, then Wells when Logan had moved in with and married a woman he'd met only a few months before. The job became her entire life, and soon her parents had stopped calling; her friends had stopped asking her out. Her partner stopped trying to talk to her on patrol. They'd all given up on her. The only one who hadn't turned away from her had been Wells, with his beautiful green eyes and chubby hands reaching for her as her ex had walked out the door with their son in his arms for the last time. And she'd just stood there. Frozen. Incapable. Weak.

But Vincent had just promised not to give up on her.

"I'm sorry for what I said. You've saved my life, I don't know how many times now, and you deserve better. I *know* the plane crash wasn't your fault, and it's not your fault I lost my son, either. I should never have put that burden on you." She nodded, lowering her gaze to the floor as she rubbed the goose pimples from her arms. Forcing herself to take a deep breath, she attempted to clear the last remnants of emotion from her system—in vain. It'd been so long since she'd been able to feel anything, she wasn't sure how to control her emotions anymore. If she could at all. "The truth is I'm the reason my ex started seeing another woman during our marriage, why he filed for divorce. And why he took Wells from me."

The weight of his attention settled on her chest, a physical presence she couldn't ignore. "He cheated on you?"

The anger in his voice rocketed her awareness into overdrive.

"Yes, but my point is… I wouldn't be here without you, and if trusting you gets me to my son, then that's what I'll do." Hell, did any of this make sense to him? She swiped her hand across her forehead. She shrugged despite the battle that'd been raging inside for so long. "Everything else…none of it matters."

"It matters to me." Vincent clasped his big hands around hers, invigorating her senses with a fresh wave of his wild, masculine scent. "Your ex-husband has to be the stupidest man on the planet to push an incredible, strong, determined woman like you out of his life. It doesn't matter what reason he had. You are worthy of a man who will treat you with the care and respect you deserve. Someone who will stand by your side, no matter what. Who will protect you until his last breath and risk his life to be with you."

All too easily, she imagined Vincent as that man, the one who would wake her and Wells with breakfast in the mornings before he headed into the office for his next assignment, the one who'd spoil her to the ends of the earth with attention and love, the one who'd place a flower over her left ear to announce to his family he'd claimed her body, mind and spirit. She swayed at the intensity of the fantasy, at how incredibly real it was. At how much she wanted it to be true, but this, being stranded out here with him, it was about survival. Nothing more. Because there couldn't be anything more with her. Not anymore.

"I'm not the person you think I am, Vincent." Shea tugged her hands out of his. She'd already hit rock bottom over the past few months. What more could she have to lose by telling him the truth, by telling him that despite that gut-wrenching kiss and explaining the way he made her feel, nothing could happen between them? It was sweet the way he'd stood up for her, called her strong when she'd convinced herself otherwise the past nine months. But in reality, he was only able to see what she'd wanted him to see. What she'd wanted everyone to see, including herself. That strength, the determination? None of it was real.

Vincent studied her with those incredibly dark, sexy eyes and her nerve endings fired in rapid succession, keeping her in the moment. Would he still look at her as though she were the only woman in the world after he learned the truth? That she was broken? That she wasn't worthy of all those things he'd described? "You have this picture of this immovable, dedicated public servant, mother and wife in your head, but it's all wrong. I'm not that woman." Shea dropped her gaze to the dimly lit floor, unable to stand another second of his worshipful attention. "You have no idea how much I wish I was her, but a woman like that doesn't cut herself off from everyone she loves. I'm not anything remotely close to that."

"You are to me." He tucked his knuckle under her chin, forcing her to look up at him, and every nerve ending she had responded. "Nothing you say is going to convince me otherwise."

Chapter Six

Cold worked its way under his heavy jacket as Vincent dropped the magazine out of their only weapon, checked the rounds and slammed it back into place. The sun had gone down, and his fingers numbed with temperatures dropping by the second. The trap was set, but he had yet to see any movement from the surrounding trees. Shea had drifted off to sleep in the only bed in the station about an hour ago, and he'd offered to take the first shift on patrol. He couldn't sleep. Not with their last conversation echoing through his head. He might've worked forensics for most of his career, but he'd read the truth easily enough: Shea didn't believe she was worthy of love. Not just from her ex-husband—the cheating bastard—but from her son, from her friends, family. Everyone in her life. She'd severed her connections to the people she was supposed to care about.

And he wanted to know why.

He'd gotten his hands on her case files before they'd started working together with permission of the Anchorage PD's chief of police, studied the way Shea worked, if she stayed within the lines of the law as she claimed. There'd been a few close calls on the job, mostly domestic disputes that hadn't ended when she and her partner had arrived on the scene. One armed robbery in which she'd intercepted the getaway driver at gunpoint. Nothing to make him think something had drastically altered her life or would dictate how close she got to those she cared about the most. There was no doubt she loved her son. He'd seen her desperation to get Wells back from her ex-husband, how missing the custody hearing was tearing her apart from the inside. So what could've possibly happened for her to believe she didn't deserve to be happy, to be loved?

A branch shifted off to his right, and Vincent homed in on the movement. Waited.

A wall of muscle slammed into him from the opposite side of the clearing, knocking the air from his lungs, and he landed face-first in two feet of snow. Twisting, he grabbed a handful and tossed it into the face of the man who'd tackled him and took aim. His attacker grabbed the weapon and slammed it into Vincent's face. Once. Twice. Vincent blocked the third attempt, but, faster than he thought possible, the gun disappeared into the trees. White stars flashed in the corners of his eyes as he raised his fists. It'd take a lot more than a couple hits to the face to bring him down. His heart threatened to pound straight out of his chest as Vincent lunged, slamming his opponent into a nearby tree. Flakes fell around them, blocking his view of his attacker, as he clamped his grip around the bastard's throat. A knee to his kidney sent pain ricocheting through his entire right side, and his hold loosened. The station blurred in his vision as the SOB landed a solid hook to his jaw.

Movement registered as he straightened, closing in on either side of the cabin. Damn it. The bastard hadn't come alone. Sliding his index fingers between his lips, he whistled as loud as he could to give his partner warning. Shea. He had to get to Shea. He pushed his hair out of his vision, facing off with the first attacker once again. He couldn't let them breach the station. Pulling the small blade at his ankle, Vincent swiped high. His opponent threw himself backward, thrown off-balance, and Vincent rushed forward to strike again. Pain exploded through his right shoulder as a bullet tore through muscle and tissue from behind, and his scream filled the clearing. He clung to the wound as he spun toward the newest threat, switching the blade to his other hand. He threw it end over end as hard as he could.

The knife penetrated the gunman's coat and brought the shooter to his knees. One down, three to go. Blood trickled beneath his jacket down his hand as he turned back in time for the original attacker to close the space between them. Vincent hiked his injured shoulder back, ignoring the pain shooting through his nerve endings as a guttural growl worked up his throat. No time to check the wound.

Smoke tainted the air a split second before the flames registered. The two operatives had made it into the station. He only hoped the trap he'd set combining gasoline and the lantern's flame when they'd barged through the front door had distracted them long enough to give Shea a way out. Vincent dodged the swipe of a much larger blade, then another. He blocked the third attempt and turned the knife back around on his attacker before sinking it deep into the man's side.

A gasp filled his ears as his opponent's legs failed him, but Vincent kept the man upright. He wasn't finished with him.

"You've got about twenty minutes before you bleed to death, and believe me, you don't want that to happen out here." Vincent strengthened his hold on the blade, both the wound in his thigh and the latest in his shoulder screaming for relief. "Tell me who sent you after me, and I'll make sure you aren't paralyzed for the rest of your life when I'm finished with you and your buddies."

"We're not only here for you, Kalani." The attacker sagged in Vincent's arms, his breath turning into shallow hisses from between his teeth. He spit a mouthful of blood into the snow, staring up at Vincent with agony contorting his expression. The man's jacket slid to one side and exposed the brass shield at his hip. "You should've left well enough alone."

"You're NYPD." Hell. The bastard confirmed his theory. The murder of the officer from the Internal Affairs Bureau had been connected to someone on the inside. Whether that meant IAB Officer Walter had been working for them was something Vincent would have to prove another day. Right now, he only had one priority: getting to Shea. He'd gotten her involved in this, and he'd get her out. Vincent pulled the knife from his attacker's side and pushed him off-balance. "You shouldn't have come after me."

His attacker hit the ground as flames inside the station broke through windows and consumed everything in its path. Two gunmen left. He swept the gun from the hole it'd made in the snow into his hand. Smoke billowed around him, and he covered his face in the crook of his elbow as he tracked a set of deep footprints around the north side of the ranger station. Heat seared his exposed skin, sweat building at the base of his spine as he maneuvered around the flames, but he'd push through the memories racing to the front of his mind. This wasn't New York City. He wasn't trapped by the fire here. Although the situations were more similar than he cared to admit.

The trap had done its job. First, to incapacitate the two remaining gunmen hunting them, and second, to signal fire and rescue. With their luck, emergency personnel was already on their way. Shea had been instructed to head west as soon as she escaped the station, to another ranger station they'd located on a map inside about three miles from here. Now he just had to find her and take down anyone still on her trail.

"Vincent." That voice. *Her* voice. "Don't come any closer."

He slowed, every muscle down his back tensing for battle as he took in the sight of her. Blood dripped down her nose and mouth, those impossibly green eyes even brighter in the flames. Gunmen flanked her on either side, weapons aimed at her midsection. Tendrils of her hair clung to her skin, the glow of the fire accentuating the freckles across her nose and cheeks. She hadn't gotten away. A soft buzzing filled his ears as he curled his hand around the gun. "She has nothing to do with this. You came for me. Let her go, and you can have me."

"What?" Shea tried to rip her arm from one man's grip, but he held on tight. "No."

"You brought her into this, Kalani. That makes her a loose end." The gunman at her right stepped forward, and a sense of recognition surfaced. Short brown hair, dark eyes, sharp features with a bristled jawline. Vincent had met this man before. But where? "You just couldn't stop yourself from looking into that IAB officer's death, even after we gave you a second chance." He jerked Shea into his chest and pressed a gun to her temple, and everything inside Vincent raged. "How many more people are you going to put in danger before you take a hint? First your teammates back in New York, now this one. She must not mean much if you were willing to risk her life to get what you wanted."

The opposite rang true. She was a motivating factor for him getting on that damn plane, the reason he didn't want to spend the rest of his life looking over his shoulder. She was...everything. His attention slid to Shea, to her almost imperceptible nod as the station burned behind him, and the pressure behind his sternum reached full capacity. "You have no idea who you're dealing with."

An evil smile stretched the gunman's mouth, and a flash of memory darted across his mind. His stomach dropped out as Vincent realized where he'd met this man before. The last homicide he'd worked... The gunman had been at the outer perimeter but inside the crime scene tape taking statements from witnesses. "I've done my research on you, Kalani. I think I'll take my chances."

The bastard was a cop, same as his attacker bleeding out on the other side of the station. Vincent studied the second gunman, caught the briefest hint of the SIG SAUER similar to his old service weapon. They were all cops. NYPD, if he had to guess. Alaska was far outside the lines of their jurisdiction, which meant the squad wasn't here in an official capacity. He locked his gaze on Shea. The tactical team that'd been hunting them these past two days was made up of corrupt NYPD officers.

"I wasn't talking about me." Vincent lunged forward, targeting the attacker on her right as Shea threw her elbow back into the man at her left. In an instant, he'd closed the distance between him and the first gunman. A bullet ripped past his ear as he collided with the cop, taking them both down. He hauled back his injured shoulder and launched his fist into the officer's face to finish the job.

Shea's sharp groan pulled at his attention from behind. The second gunman stood over her, and a predatory growl was torn from Vincent's throat. Nobody put their hands on her. No one. He shoved to his feet, but he'd made it only one step before something hard slammed against his head. He collapsed into the snow, pitched into darkness.

HER FACE THROBBED. Shea blinked against the sudden brightness around her as her body jerked to a stop. Hot. Why was it so hot? She'd spent the past two days chilled to the bone, but now sweat built beneath her heavy clothing. She tugged at the zip ties around her wrists and ankles. Ringing filled her ears as she twisted her head to one side, to the trees within arm's reach. Her last memories played across her mind in flashes and tensed the muscles down her spine. She'd been knocked unconscious. The tactical team had found them, and she'd barely escaped the station before the old wood floor had caught fire from Vincent's trap. She hiked her head back over her shoulder, snow crunching beneath the crown of her head. Now two members of that same team were hefting something heavy closer to the flames destroying the ranger station. The air rushed out of her lungs, but she bit back the scream caught in her throat. Not something. Vincent.

"Boss said destroy the evidence. Then we can get the hell out of here," one of them said.

No. Shea rolled onto one side, feeling for something—anything—she could use to break the zip ties. Her fingers sorted through loose rock, chunks of ice and broken twigs from the trees above. Eyes on both men, she slowly sat up and fisted a large piece of ice from beneath the powder. If the edge was sharp enough, it'd cut through the plastic. Unless the heat from her hands melted it first. She placed the icy blade's edge between her feet and started sawing at the ties around her ankles. Fire crackled and popped from less than ten feet away, her skin burning hot to the point she had to turn away to protect her face.

Pain pulsed across her cheek from where the second gunman had struck her, but she pushed it to the back of her mind as ice turned to water in her hands. Damn it. The ice was melting too fast. She wouldn't be able to get both her hands and her ankles free at this pace. Not before the gunmen dragged Vincent into the flames. She worked faster, harder. She strengthened her grip around the melting weapon as desperation clawed up her throat and clenched her back teeth against the numbness in her hand. "Come on."

The zip tie snapped from around her feet, but relief was short-lived. A shadow crossed over her, instantly cooling her exposed skin.

"Well, well, well. Looks like we've got ourselves a fighter here." The gunman, the one who'd knocked her unconscious, wrapped a strong grip around her arm and wrenched Shea to her feet. The sting of too much cologne burned her nostrils as he pulled her into his chest. Perfectly straight white teeth battled with the sneer stretching the man's cracked lips wide. His bruising hold on her arm increased as she maneuvered her bound wrists between their bodies. "I've always liked a challenge."

"Then you're going to love me." Shea brought up her hands, striking him right in the face as hard as she could. Her knuckles tingled with the hit, but she struck again. The gunman stumbled back, and she followed but didn't catch him drawing a blade in time before stinging pain exploded across her arm. She blocked the next swing and clamped both hands on to his forearm as she rammed her knee into his kidney. Once. Twice. He lost the knife, then she used his own fist to follow through with another punch to his face, knocking him unconscious. Shea dived for the blade as her attacker collapsed at her feet and cut through the ties at her wrists. She unholstered the gun at his hip, catching sight of the NYPD badge on the other side of his belt.

The men who'd attacked them, brought down the plane, they were…cops.

Breathing heavy, vision blurred, she reached out to the nearest tree to keep her balance. She took aim at the first gunman near Vincent as he unholstered his weapon. "Drop the gun and get your hands up where I can see them."

"Gotta say I'm impressed, Officer Ramsey." His voice sent an uncontrollable quake down through her as he raised both arms above his head, gun still in hand. One shot. That was all it would take to rip the man who'd helped bring her back to life away, but she'd pull this trigger just as quickly. "Although we've gotten close over the past hour, so I feel like I should call you Shea."

Her stomach lurched. Whether from the possible concussion or the fact that the man pointing a gun at Vincent had done his research, she didn't know. Her attention dipped to Vincent, to the slight rise and fall of his chest. He was alive. She still had a chance to get them out of here. She caught sight of their supply bag where their attackers had thrown it after intercepting her dash into the trees. She hadn't been fast enough, but she wouldn't make that mistake again. "Is the fact that you know my name supposed to scare me?"

"I could've gotten your name off the plane's passenger manifest or threatened to shoot your pilot unless he gave me the names of his passengers, but I didn't have to do either of those things." The gunman shook his head, dark eyes glittering with help from the fire. A humorless laugh burst from his Kevlar-covered chest. "We found out you've been partnering with Vincent here for a few months when we stopped in to check up on him. I got the feeling he wasn't going to heed our warning to back off his…independent investigation into a case from back home, maybe even trusted someone here with the intel he thought he had. Turns out, I was right. Then I find out you're on the same plane he is heading to New York, and that gets me thinking. Vincent could've been trying to use Anchorage PD resources to find out who killed his IAB friend. And, well, we can't have that." He waved the gun toward her, and she slipped her finger over the trigger of her own weapon. "I know what kind of cop you are, Shea. I know there's nothing I can say to get you to walk away now. So instead of coming in here and trying to convince you to forget you ever saw us, I had my guys in New York pay a visit to your ex."

The blood drained from her face. Logan? Her heart pounded hard in her chest, threatening to burst through her rib cage. She swiped her tongue across her lips to counter the sudden dryness in her throat. It was a manipulation, a desperate measure to get her to believe he had leverage over her. These dirty cops had come for Vincent, and she had no doubt in her mind they'd say anything to get what they wanted. But they couldn't have him. Her arms shook with the weight of the gun in her hand, but she held strong. "I said drop the gun."

"I get it. Exes are exes for a reason, right? You probably don't feel the same way about him as you would about, say, that little boy of yours." That smile was back, and her gut knotted tight. "What was his name?" The gunman lowered his hands slowly, and Shea stepped forward in warning. A slight pull at one corner of his mouth accentuated the sharp angles of his face. "Wells, right? Cute kid. It'd be a shame if he got caught in the middle of what we have going on here." The gunman nudged Vincent with his boot. "It's too late for your partner here, but you can still walk away. You can go to New York and get your son back. That's what you want, right? I can make that happen. All you have to do is stand down, Officer Ramsey."

He was threatening her son. Threatening Vincent. Seconds slipped by. A minute. She had a chance to get to Wells, to fight for him as she should've done in the first place. Sweat fell from her temples, her hands damp against the gun's grip.

All she had to do was walk away. The fire had destroyed the ranger station in a matter of minutes and had started spreading to the nearby tree line. A groan reached her ears from behind. The attacker she'd taken down was coming around. She was out of time.

"I swore an oath to protect and serve." Shea lowered her weapon, shortened her shooting stance. Made herself a smaller target. Her gaze dropped to Vincent as his hand splayed across the white snow, leaving a print of red behind. He'd been injured trying to protect her, and every cell in her body screamed in retaliation. The man giving her the chance to run was a cop. His entire squad was made of cops, but they weren't playing by the rules. She wasn't an officer out here. She didn't have the manpower to arrest these men. So maybe Vincent had been right. Maybe the rules didn't always apply, and he and his team weren't the vigilantes she'd believed. She lifted her gaze to the gunman. "And that's exactly what I'm going to do."

Shea raised the gun and fired.

Vincent's attacker pulled the trigger at the same time his shoulder ripped back from the impact of her shot, but his bullet went wide. He fell with a pain-filled scream, the sound echoing off the rock around them.

"Vincent!" She dashed toward him, gun still in hand, and tugged him to his feet. Taking the majority of his weight, Shea half dragged him to their discarded supply bag and then into the tree line just as the second gunman got to his feet. Her attacker ran for his superior, taking up a nearby weapon as she hauled Vincent to her side. "Come on, we've got to get out of here."

Three shots exploded from behind, but she kept them moving. Blood trickled down onto her hand from his shoulder as she fought to keep Vincent upright. The faster they ran, the faster he'd bleed, but they couldn't stop. Couldn't look back. No matter what happened next, they were in this together.

Chapter Seven

Shea had chosen him.

His vision blurred as they stumbled through the trees, gunmen once again on their trail. Three miles of wilderness and bullets stood between them and the next ranger station, but Shea had taken her chances with him. Given up a shot at seeing her son again to save his life. Vincent pitched forward as another surge of pain crushed the air from his lungs. The bullet was still inside his shoulder, tearing through muscle and tissue. Every swing of his arm, every brush with the trees, was another lesson in pain tolerance, but he couldn't give away their position. Distraction. He needed a distraction. "You could've walked away."

"What kind of person do you think I am? I wasn't going to leave you with them to die." Her heavy breathing hitched as she checked back over her shoulder, the gun still in her free hand. The glow of the fire lit her eyes in an unnatural display of brightness, and Vincent couldn't look away. "I think you were right. The IAB officer's murder you were looking into in New York goes a lot deeper than the investigating officers reported. The men trying to kill us are cops."

"They're corrupt cops. Part of an organization inside the NYPD I've only heard rumors about until now. Back in New York, I collected evidence from four different homicide scenes that'd been cleaned a bit too well, like the perp knew how to hide evidence. I even found proof a detective had broken into a witness's home in order to intimidate her to drop a complaint against his partner. They're not just cops. They're hit men, but these guys won't answer to just anyone." He locked his jaw against the shooting pain all along the right side of his body as deep snow jerked him down. The shrapnel in his thigh, a bullet in his shoulder and the hit to his head from behind. He was lucky he was still standing. Lucky to be alive. Vincent tried to keep most of his weight off of Shea, but any extraneous shifting on his part only increased the discomfort. Hell, he wouldn't be here if it wasn't for her. "They've got to have a superior officer giving orders. Someone in the NYPD who needed to cover up IAB Officer Walter's murder and put out the hit on me and my team that night. I'm going to find out who."

"The NYPD is made up of over fifty thousand officers and civilian employees," she said. "It could be anyone."

"I didn't say it would be easy." Numbness spread from his toes up his calves. The sun had gone down hours ago; every exhale froze instantaneously on the air. If they couldn't make it to the next station, there was a chance they'd die out here. Vincent slowed. "Why did you do it?"

He didn't have to elaborate. They both knew he wanted to know why she'd given up the promise of seeing her son again in order to save his life.

"They've already killed our pilot, an innocent man who, as far as we know, had nothing to do with your case in New York. I don't care what they were promising. They weren't going to let me walk away. Not after I'd seen their faces." She redirected her attention to the darkness growing behind them. Her voice hardened, the muscles along her jawline flexing in the dim light from their flashlight. "But I pulled the trigger because he threatened my son. I wanted him to realize he'd made a mistake bringing Wells into this."

"I think he got the message." Vincent put more pressure on his injured leg but kept his arm around her shoulders for support. How the hell had she dragged him at least half a mile through the wilderness without showing a hint of exhaustion in her features? She was strong, stronger than he'd originally estimated, but small cracks had begun to surface back at that station. She blamed herself for her divorce, for losing custody of her son to her ex, but when it'd come down to the wire, she'd stepped in to protect a man she'd resented from day one from a group of corrupt cops. She'd been right before. She wasn't the woman he'd built up in his mind. She was better. "Whatever the reason, thank you."

The growl of a distant engine reached through the trees.

"That sounds like an ATV," she said.

And it was closing in.

They didn't have much time before the cops who'd shot him headed them off. It'd be easy to track his and Shea's path through the snow, but ATVs couldn't navigate through these trees. Hell only knew how many of them were out there now, on foot. "That would explain how they found the plane so quickly. We wouldn't have been able to hear the engines from the amount of snow blocking the entrance of the cave."

"I thought it'd take them longer to regroup." Shea rubbed her hands together, then swiped her hand across her face. She tucked the gun into the back of her jeans and covered it with her coat, all the while never taking her arm from around his lower back. "These guys are persistent. I'll give them that."

"Which means we can't go to the next ranger station. They'll be waiting for us there." If they weren't already. He couldn't take the chance. Not after Shea had risked her life to save his. He'd promised to get her to New York to fight for her son, and he had no intention of failing her again. "We have to go deeper into the woods. North. They won't be looking for us there."

"Every minute we spend out here is another chance we don't make it out of these mountains." Wide eyes searched his face. "If we head north, we'll just be saving the guys with the guns the trouble when we die out here from exposure."

"I know what I'm asking of you, Shea." He'd never wanted any of this, but it was the only way. "We have to take the risk. Otherwise, they'll shoot us on sight. I need you to trust me." They still had their supply pack with the extra food she'd packaged and plenty of fresh snow to keep hydrated. The problem would be heat. They'd used all of the kindling he'd had and lighting a fire would only give away their position, and any they found out here would be too wet to catch fire. If they were going to make it through the night, they'd have to rely on each other. Trust each other. Completely. Vincent lowered his voice. This was it. This was the moment that would either drive them apart or bring them together. There was no going back. "We survive together."

"Or we die alone." With a small nod, Shea adjusted her hold around his back and brought him into her side. Her body heat seeped through his coat down into muscle. Her rich scent gathered at the back of his throat as they moved north through the trees as one in some kind of demented three-legged race. Only this race was for their lives. "I hope you're right about this."

"Me, too." Vincent couldn't let his past ruin her future. He'd never forgive himself for tearing apart her life. Not when she'd risked everything to save him back there at the ranger station. But even before then, he'd known he'd do whatever it took to ensure she made it out of this alive. She had to. For the innocents she protected, for her family. For him.

A grouping of flashlight beams bounced in the distance.

Vincent instantly killed theirs to stay hidden but kept them moving. Damn it. How many of them were out there? A dozen? More? He spun them northeast and took a step forward. More flash-lights. He turned back the way they'd come and froze. Shea's uneven breathing registered in the darkness as the lights danced around them.

"We're surrounded." She'd lowered her voice to avoid giving away their position, but it wouldn't do a damn bit of good. The corrupt officers he'd worked to expose back in New York had found them.

But he and Shea weren't dead. Not yet. He could still get her out of this mess. The flashlight beams steadied as the hit men carrying them slowed, closing the circle around them. His eyes had already adjusted to the darkness. He counted eleven hostiles, all heavily armed, and stepped away from Shea as every muscle along his spine contracted with battle-ready tension. A chance to escape. That was all he needed to give her. Vincent slipped his hand beneath the seam of her coat, over the gun at her back, but didn't draw. Any movement on their part could be his and Shea's last, but he wasn't finished with her yet. He studied the single officer stepping forward from the circle of cops, the one Shea had shot back at the station. The SOB's name had pierced through the haze as he'd watched her pull the trigger. Officer Charles Grillo.

"I gave you the chance to walk away, Officer Ramsey, and you shot me." Grillo raised his weapon, aimed directly at Shea. The flashlight beams highlighted the blood spreading across the officer's coat a split second before he pulled the trigger.

She wrenched back, her scream loud in his ears as Shea hit the ground.

"No!" Vincent crouched over her, applying pressure to the wound in her side. Her breathing shallow, her eyes shut tight as she fought against the pain of the bullet tearing through her. Rage—unlike anything he'd felt before—surfaced in a dark, overwhelming current. He focused on Grillo as he suffocated the agony from the shot to his shoulder. The cold had slowed the bleeding, numbed the area around the wound, but now he felt everything. "You're going to die for that, Officer Grillo."

"You got her involved in this. Not me. You could've walked away, started your life over, but instead you decided you wanted to play the hero." The officer swung the barrel of his weapon at Vincent. "We already know about Officer Ramsey here. Who else did you bring into your investigation?"

Containment. That was the only reason he and Shea were still alive. Whoever'd sent these bastards wanted to ensure nobody else had gotten hold of the evidence from Officer Ashton Walter's death scene. Otherwise, Vincent had the feeling Grillo and his team of corrupt cops would've already disposed of their bodies. Blood welled between his fingers as he increased the pressure on Shea's wound. She wasn't struggling anymore, her breathing slow. He'd run that print through the Integrated Automated Fingerprint Identification System—IAFIS—with the help of Blackhawk's network security analyst, which meant his entire Blackhawk team could be at risk now. Because of him. "Go to hell."

He wrapped his fingers around Shea's service weapon, drew and fired.

GUNSHOTS EXPLODED FROM all around.

Shea forced her eyes open, but the haze at the edges of her vision threatened to pull her into unconsciousness. More shots echoed through the night, shadows shifting around her. She couldn't make out anything distinctive. The ringing in her ears was too loud to discern the shouts, but the feel of her weapon at her back was gone. Vincent. He must've taken her gun. Curls slid into her vision as she turned on her side. Clamping her hand over the wound, she pushed upright. Lightning fired through her pain receptors, and she ducked her chin to her chest to keep the scream working up her throat at bay. Where was he?

Chaos pulled her attention to the broken ring of gunmen as another round of bullets pierced the night. Getting to her feet, Shea stumbled forward, free hand outstretched as her boot collided with something heavy and unmoving in the snow.

Rocking back on her heels, she landed on her butt in the powder. She clawed for the flashlight discarded a few feet away and swept it over the body, her throat tight. Instant relief coursed through her. One of the gunmen. Not Vincent. She collected the officer's weapon and killed the flashlight beam. He was out there, taking on an entire ring of corrupt cops on his own. He needed help.

Shea straightened again, hugging her arm into her side, and took cover behind the nearest tree. There. Another gunshot exploded from nearby and a flashlight hit the ground. Several more closed in on the shooter's position, and she turned to approach the group from behind.

Stinging agony spread across her scalp as a fist clenched her hair, her back hitting solid muscle and a wall of Kevlar.

"Where do you think you're going?" The man Vincent had called Grillo shoved her forward, and she hit the ground face-first. "You're as much a part of this as your partner is now, and we're not done."

Ice worked beneath the collar of her coat and T-shirt, shocking her into action. Shea flipped over just as he lunged for her again and rolled out of his reach but lost her newly acquired gun in the snow. The wound in her side screamed in protest, but she forced herself to get back to her feet. He came at her, his fist aimed directly for her face. Dodging the first attempt to knock her out, she slammed her forearm into his as he tried again, but she wasn't fast enough to block his free hand. Bone met the flesh of her face. The momentum of his hit twisted her head to the side, her eyes watering from the hit, but she kept upright. Copper and salt filled her mouth. She spit the blood, the inside of her cheek stinging where her teeth had cut into the soft tissue.

"You shouldn't have sided with Kalani, Officer Ramsey," he said. "Because now I'm going to have to hurt you."

Dread curled at the base of her stomach. This man had access to her son. And no matter which way she looked at it, as a mother, as an officer, she couldn't let him leave this clearing. Not without risking him contacting the men he had watching Wells. Shea shot her fist forward, connecting with one temple, then landed a kick center mass to his chest before he could recover. "And you shouldn't have gone after my son."

Grillo stumbled back, but didn't go down, and she raised her fists for another attack. Unsheathing a knife in one hand, her attacker tried to circle around her position. He rushed forward, the knife leading the way, and the snow slowed her down. The tip of the knife cut through her thick coat and sliced across her upper arm. "You have no idea how much I'm going to enjoy this."

Another wave of pain helped her forget the bullet that had embedded in her midsection. She wrapped her numb fingers around his wrist as he lunged forward again, maneuvered behind him, and put as much pressure as she could manage against his injured arm. He let go of the knife as she forced him to double over, the weight on his elbow too much to do anything else. With enough pressure, she'd do irreparable damage. Her heart pounded hard in her chest. Blood pooled beneath her clothing, dripping into the waistband of her jeans. "Call off your men." Only his breathing registered, and she applied more pressure. His groan heightened the effects of the nausea swirling in her gut. She didn't like hurting people. She'd sworn to protect them, but she wouldn't let Vincent die out here while he fought to protect her. "Now."

A rumble of laughter vibrated through Grillo's chest and into her grip on his arm. "You going to kill me, Ramsey? Because that's the only way you're walking out of here. That's the only way you're going to save your son before my guys get to him."

She didn't get a chance to respond as Grillo swung his opposite hand up, grabbed on to her neck, and slammed her into the ground. The air crushed from her lungs, the darkness threatening to consume her all over again. Her head pounded in rhythm to her racing heartbeat as his shadow moved over her, but she wasn't going to die here. Shea kicked out, catching him in the stomach, and clawed for the gun she'd lost a few minutes ago. The metal chilled her hand as she brought it out in front of her and aimed. Her chest heaved as her lungs fought to catch up with the rest of her body. "Don't move."

"You already shot me once, Ramsey. You sure as hell better make sure you kill me this time." Grillo took a step forward, and she pulled the trigger.

Nothing happened.

She tried again, and again, but the gun wouldn't fire. Her lips parted. No. No, no, no, no. Silence descended. Ice worked through her veins, and it had nothing to do with the dropping temperatures. Raising her gaze to Grillo's, she caught the hint of a smile thinning his lips.

"Now it's my turn." He unholstered a hidden weapon from his lower back, centering her in his crosshairs, and her insides clenched.

She'd been on the wrong end of a gun before in the line of duty, but nothing like this. No one had ever wanted to kill her, to kill one of her partners, to hurt her son. Whoever these people were work-

ing for—whoever'd sent them to kill Vincent—
they were going to get away with it if she didn't
get up. But she'd already lost too much blood. The
ringing in her ears was back, weblike patterns at
the corners of her eyes. She tried sitting up, tried
blocking the path of Grillo's bullet with one hand,
but the very idea didn't even make sense. There
was nothing she could do. She couldn't save Vincent. She couldn't save her son. She couldn't even
save herself. Just as she hadn't been able to after
giving birth to Wells.

Vincent. His name echoed in her mind, and the
fear holding her in place evaporated. The gunfire
had died down. Was he injured? Would she survive long enough to make it to him in time? The
man she'd kept at a distance due to her own private battle with the way he'd made her feel these
past few months had saved her life out here. More
times than she could count. Vincent and his team
had skirted the law when it came to their investigations time and time again, but Shea couldn't
deny the fact that they'd saved so many lives in
the process. Including hers. The thought of this
team of corrupt cops burying the forensic investigator she'd come to rely on churned her stomach.
Shea put everything she had into getting to her
feet, but it wasn't enough. Her knees buckled as

a wave of dizziness washed over her. Now it was time to save his.

"You don't know when to give up, do you, Officer Ramsey?" he asked. "Maybe you and I aren't so different after all."

"I took the same oath as you to protect the innocent. The only difference between us is I actually try to hold up my end." Shea rushed her attacker. She'd trained in active shooter situations. The best chance she had of surviving—of Vincent surviving—was to get control of that gun. Dark eyes widened a split second before a wall of muscle slammed into Grillo from the right, knocking all three of them to the ground. The trees surrounding them blurred in streaks of black and white as she rolled down an incline. A scream escaped up her throat as she slammed into a boulder mere feet from where Grillo and another man struggled to their feet. "Vincent."

She scanned the area, counted the bodies around the clearing. Ten. Not including Grillo. He'd taken them all down. Who the hell had she partnered with these past few months? Shea smothered the fear climbing up her throat. He was injured, favoring his right leg and the gunshot wound in his shoulder. Grillo shook his head as though trying to clear it and attacked. Vincent blocked the first hit, then the next, but took the third and fourth directly to the kidneys. Pressing her hand to her own wound, Shea hauled herself to her feet. Adrenaline narrowed her focus on the weapon Grillo had dropped as they'd rolled down the hill. Wrapping her hand around the grip, she brought the gun up.

"I told you I enjoyed a challenge." A hand clamped over her mouth, wrenching her back. Icy metal pressed against her temple, the scent of stale cigarettes and cologne overwhelming, and everything inside her went cold. The cop, the one who'd knocked her unconscious back at the ranger station, lowered his mouth to her ear. "I'd prefer not to put a bullet in you before I've had my chance to pay you back for the new scar to my face. Get rid of the gun."

Hesitation coursed through her, but she'd lost the upper hand. The breath rushed out of her. Tossing the weapon a few feet away, she fought back the nausea and pain swirling through her as Vincent took another hit. He collapsed to the ground, those mesmerizing brown eyes settling on her as Grillo launched his knee into Vincent's face. Her protector slumped to the ground. Out cold. Grillo gathered the discarded gun and shot Vincent two times to the chest. Center mass. Exactly as she'd been trained.

"No!" she screamed from behind the hand braced over her mouth, the sound distorted and desperate. Her legs threatened to give out as the last of her adrenaline drained. Tears burned in her eyes, and she wrenched herself out of her attacker's grasp and launched forward. Only she couldn't reach Vincent in time.

Grillo pushed her toward his partner, his grip bruising.

The officer at her back spun her around and pressed the gun's barrel to her temple once again. Those perfect white teeth flashed in a wide smile. Dried blood flaked from the laceration at his temple where she'd hit him as Grillo circled around to face her. "Let's talk about what's going to happen next, Officer Ramsey."

Chapter Eight

Vincent sat up, gasping for air. His lungs protested the sharp bite of cold as pain radiated outward from the two slugs Grillo had buried dead center in his chest. He locked his jaw against the groan in his throat as he battled to stay upright. Hell, it was hard to breathe with this damn thing on. Not to mention the impact of two bullets to the chest. Leveraging his back against the nearest tree, he closed his eyes against the soreness as he unzipped his heavy coat to examine the damage. A combination of pink and orange filtered across the sky, giving him enough light to pick one crumpled bullet from the Kevlar vest. The metal was still warm to the touch. Patterns in the snow a few feet away demanded his attention. Divots cut a path around him, south through the trees. And blood. His gut clenched as he crawled the few feet between him and the drops. Shea.

They couldn't have gotten far. If he hurried, he

still might be able to save her. He'd gotten Shea into this mess. He'd fight to get her out of it, but more than that, he couldn't stand the thought of working with a new partner on the department's joint investigations with Blackhawk. Couldn't stand the thought of losing her. Not when he was beginning to break past those icy barriers and see the vulnerable, fiery, secretive woman beneath. They'd survived this long as a team. He wasn't about to give that up.

Struggling to his feet, he ignored the slight drag of his right leg and the throbbing in his shoulder as he patted down one of the men he'd taken down. He unholstered an extra weapon, checked the magazine, and loaded a round into the chamber. Numbness had worked through his fingers and toes, but oddly, the rest of his body was slick with sweat. These bastards had taken her, and he was going to get her back. Then he'd hunt down the SOB who'd ordered Grillo and his team to take him out. "Hold on for me, Shea."

He followed the droplets of blood until the trees thinned, every cell in his body screaming in protest. The faster his heart pumped, the more blood he'd lose, but he wouldn't stop because his body was tired. Only when the job was done. The trail ended at the bank of a frozen lake nestled between two mountains, but there was nothing but open views and thick ice out here. Pops and cracks echoed in his ears. Grillo wouldn't have crossed the lake with a hostage in tow. Not with these open sight lines and the chance of falling through the ice. Too risky. Realization hit as strong as another shot to the chest as he turned to study the trail. "The bastard must've doubled back."

He'd been following a dummy trail, made to look as though the corrupt SOBs who'd taken Shea had come this way. Puffs of air crystalized in front of his mouth. Damn it. He had to stay dry. Any hint of moisture led to hypothermia, and Shea was already running out of time.

Movement caught his attention from behind, and Vincent swung around, gun at the ready. Grillo's partner—the one who'd taken Shea at gunpoint—latched onto his wrist and slammed Vincent into the nearest tree. The bastard went for the weapon, and Vincent let him as he swung a hard left directly into his attacker's face, followed by a kick to the gut. The partner stumbled back with a groan, but recovered fast, trying to deliver the same kick. Only he missed. One hit to the kidneys knocked the guy off-balance, but the next to the cop's collarbone resulted in a sickening crack of bone. The attacker's scream pierced the silence as snow fell from the sky. Threading his fingers between Grillo's partner's, he twisted the bastard's hand backward and brought the cop to his knees. "Where is she?"

Laughter mixed with a pain-filled moan. The dirty cop spit blood into the snow a few feet away. "Interrogate me all you want, Kalani. I'm not giving you a damn thing."

Light from the auroras above glinted off a hint of steel a moment before pain seared across Vincent's leg. He released his hold on the SOB but closed the space between them fast. Dodging the next swipe, he pushed the man's arm away with one hand and slammed his palm into the bastard's broken clavicle with the other. Grillo's partner dropped to one knee. Swiping the gun from the snow, Vincent crouched, pressing the barrel to the cop's temple. Just as he'd done to Shea before Vincent had been knocked unconscious. He ripped the badge off the man's waistband, the nickel silver heavy in his hand. City of New York Police. Detective. A humorless laugh escaped Vincent's bruised chest, resurrecting the ache from the two rounds Grillo had shot into the vest. He'd had a shield almost exactly like this. Before he'd lost everything.

Vincent tossed the detective's badge into the snow. "You know, back in New York, my forensic team and I were called out on a handful of homicides that made us believe the perps had to have knowledge of crime scenes. Everything had been wiped down. The bodies had been moved from one location to the other, which made it nearly impossible to identify the original crime scene, or we couldn't even identify the victims because there was barely anything left to identify. Evidence connected to the cases even started going missing from lockup, which led me to believe the killer had to be law enforcement."

Vincent studied the deep laceration on the side of the cop's head, right where Shea had knocked the jerk out cold, and a rush of satisfaction washed over him. "Of course, I couldn't prove it. You and your buddies back there in that clearing had done too good a job, and nobody up the chain of command wanted to hear that their own officers were involved in the very homicides we were trying to solve." He crouched beside Grillo's partner. "So I took my theory to Internal Affairs. I'm guessing when Officer Walter got too close to identifying the cops involved, your boss had him killed, right? But not before someone tortured him to the point he gave up the source of his intel. Me. That's why you tried to have me killed, isn't it? Only there's something you and your buddies here are forgetting, Detective."

He lowered his voice as the rage he'd caged all these months started to break through the cracks. "I was one of the best forensic investigators in the country, and I know exactly how to dispose of your body without leaving any evidence behind. Your family won't ever know what happened to you when I'm done." A flash of fear contorted the detective's face as Vincent released the safety on the weapon. "So I'm only going to ask you one more time before I pull this trigger. Where is Shea Ramsey?"

"Grillo didn't tell me where he was taking her." Panic outlined the tendons between the cop's neck and shoulders as though he expected the bullet to come next. "He left me here to take care of you in case you came after us again, but I swear I don't know where she is now. Said the less I know, the less could be tied back to us in case Blackhawk Security or Anchorage PD started looking for her. We had orders…that's all. None of this was personal, Kalani. I swear." The guy closed his eyes as Vincent increased the pressure of the gun against his head, hands raised in surrender. The bastard had to know something—anything—that could get him to Shea. "Go on, do it. If you don't kill me, if they think I gave you anything, they'll go after my kid."

The inferno burning through him cooled in an instant, and the gun's barrel slipped down a few centimeters as he processed each word out of his attacker's mouth. "What'd you say?"

His expression smoothed as he opened one eye, then the other, to stare up at Vincent. "The people I work for, they'll go after my kid if you don't kill me."

The same way they'd go after Shea's son if she didn't walk away. Grillo had been in touch with the men watching Wells back in New York. Which meant his team had to have a satellite phone or radio that worked out here between the mountains. If he could get his hands on it, he and Shea had a chance to call in backup and send one of Blackhawk's operatives to intercept the men sitting on the boy. The scent of smoke clung to his coat and hair as he forced himself to breathe evenly. Vincent adjusted his grip around the gun, finger positioned alongside the trigger. "Which direction did Grillo take her?"

"Out there." He motioned with his chin out across the lake.

The pops and cracks he'd heard before... They hadn't been the lake naturally settling. They'd been initiated by the extra weight of two adults moving across the surface of the ice. Vincent lowered the weapon to his side. What exactly had been Grillo's plan? Kill her, then drop her body beneath the ice? Despite popular belief that water washed away evidence, the freezing temperatures would only preserve it out here. Only no one would know where to look for her. Not even the most aggressive district attorney would be able to charge Grillo with first-degree murder without a body. No. He couldn't think like that. Because if he lost her... If he didn't get the chance to tell her what he'd been afraid to admit over the past few months—how she'd been the source of his need to finally solve this case—he feared he'd never stop hunting the SOBs who'd started this war in the first place. He refocused on the detective at his feet. "You're going to want to take some pain medication when you wake up."

Confusion contorted the cop's expression. "What—"

Vincent slammed the butt of the gun into the base of his attacker's neck and let him collapse forward. The bastard would wake up with a hell of a headache, but he'd live long enough to get his kid to safety. He trusted the guy could find his way back to the city. Right now, he had to get to Shea. Holstering the weapon at the small of his back, he put his weight back into his heels as he descended toward the lake's shoreline and stepped onto the ice.

One more step.

The ice groaned and snapped under her weight, dendritic patterns spreading out from where her boots landed. An ache flared as Grillo pressed the gun into her back. They must've walked at least half a mile by now. How much farther did he expect her to go with a gunshot in her side? If he didn't kill her soon, the blood loss from her wound or hypothermia settling in would do the job for him. Maybe that was his plan. Other than the bullet lodged inside her, not even the best forensic investigator in the world would be able to tie her death back to him or his ring of dirty cops, but he could remove the slug easily enough. When she wasn't able to fight back. Shea blinked to clear the haze clouding her vision. One more step. She only had to make it one more step.

"How much farther?" She dared a glance over her shoulder, back toward her attacker as her boot skidded across the surface of the lake. Throwing her bloodied hands out for balance, she held her breath until the world righted. Her body ached, her head hurt, and her heart…she'd just watched it take two bullets to the chest in her defense. Vincent. She cleared the tears—the memories of blood and gunpowder and pain—and forced herself to keep moving forward. The hole she'd struggled to patch over the last nine months after losing her son had ripped wider and more violently than she'd expected when Grillo had pulled that trigger. And now… Now she was being led across a frozen lake threatening to engulf her at any moment with a gunman at her back.

"Until I say stop." Grillo knocked her forward, and her palms hit the ice hard.

She skidded to a stop, exhales ricocheting back into her face. Cold burned the exposed skin of her palms, but she didn't have the energy to move. In the past two days her plane had gone down, she'd barely survived an avalanche and she'd been knocked unconscious and shot. How much more was she expected to endure before her body shut down completely?

"Get up." His boot nudged at her injured side.

Shea bit her tongue against the agony tearing through her, fingertips melting through the thin layer of snow that'd built between her and mere inches of ice. If Grillo pulled that trigger again, would the bullet break through? Could she force him beneath the hardened layer in a last-ditch effort to make it out of here alive? The thought penetrated through the cloudiness clinging to her brain. The effects of hypothermia had already started settling in. Confusion, slurred speech, lethargy, but the idea she could survive the organization that'd killed Vincent long enough to bring them down on her own brought clarity. In a sea of family and friends whose faces had drained of color in her fight against the postpartum depression, his had stood out in full hues. Working cases with Vincent had been a lifeline when she'd needed it the most, his challenging yet easygoing nature the only thing she'd been able to hold on to during her fight for mental health. Bringing her in on the joint investigations had saved her life in more ways than one. Physically. Mentally. Emotionally. She owed him this.

A gust of wind kicked up snow and dead foliage around her, and the hint of something clean, masculine even. She breathed it in a bit deeper, reminded of the way Vincent had so easily closed the distance between them back at the ranger station. How he'd grazed her jawline with his knuckles, resurrecting pulses of desire she'd never thought she'd feel again after her divorce. The memory of his kiss chased back the tremors racking her body now. Vincent had given his life to ensure she survived. She couldn't let it be for nothing.

"I said get up, Ramsey." Grillo fisted her hair, pulling her upper body off the ice, and her hands shot to relieve the pressure—to no avail. He was stronger than her, faster than her, but Shea wasn't going to give up. "Unless you're perfectly happy dying here. I was planning on burying you in a nice spot up here a ways, but—"

Launching her heel into his shin, she braced for impact as Grillo lost his balance and slammed down on top of her. The air crushed from her lungs, but she forced herself to her feet as his gun slid across the ice. She clawed for it, Grillo catching her ankle before she was able to reach the weapon and hit the ice again. Pain receded to the back of her mind as her fight-or-flight response focused her attention on getting free. She rocketed her heel into his nose, heard the sickening crunch, and he released his hold on her.

The ice underneath her dipped with a loud, echoing crack. Her heart rate spiked into dangerous territory as water flooded up through the crevices around her. Shea scrambled back, kicking at the ice for purchase, but it only broke apart faster.

"Shea!" Recognition flared.

In an instant, she locked on the figure running across the ice toward her. Vincent. He was alive. Fear and relief battled for supremacy as she flipped onto her stomach and dug her fingernails into the ice. A sob built in her throat, but she couldn't let the emotions tearing through her free. Not until she confirmed he was real and not some construct her mind had created in an effort for survival.

But with one more gut-wrenching crack, the surface of the lake broke. Both she and Grillo fell through, their screams cut off by ice-cold water. Every nerve ending in her body shrieked in shock as the subzero temperature paralyzed her limbs.

She couldn't think. Couldn't move. Strands of her hair blocked the view of the dim light of the auroras filtering down through the hole above, and of her attacker.

Grillo tugged her into his body, squeezing what precious oxygen she'd held on to from her chest. The bubbles tickled her overexposed skin as they raced to the surface. She targeted the gunshot in his shoulder, digging her finger into the wound, and twisted as hard as she could. His muffled scream barely reached her ears, blood spreading around them fast. She wrestled for freedom, but he only held her tighter.

The brilliant dance of lights above the surface diminished. Without air, they were sinking in a violent battle for dominance to the bottom of the lake. There were no guarantees the hole they'd fallen through would still be there when she came back up. Grillo maneuvered behind her, locking her neck in the crease of his elbow. She jerked her knee toward his head as hard as she could, but the water only slowed her momentum. Her body was growing heavier by the second, her movements rigid. This man was a corrupt cop, following someone else's orders. Was he really willing to risk his life to ensure she lost hers? Blackness clouded the corners of her vision, the cold and lack of air leaching her strength faster now, but she wouldn't give up. Couldn't. Not when she'd just started to explore the possibility of getting her son back, of moving on with her life. Of seeing if the connection between her and Vincent was real.

A shadow passed above them.

Grillo jerked behind her. His grip loosened from her neck as the water in front of her face turned red with blood.

She was still sinking, limbs refusing to respond to her brain's commands. Muscled, tattooed arms surrounded her, and her head sank back into a wall of familiar ridges and valleys. Gravity warred with the lightness overtaking her as they shot toward the opening in the ice. Below, the dark outline of her attacker faded into the deep. Her head broke through the surface, lungs automatically gasping for oxygen.

"I've got you." His voice penetrated through the erratic pounding of her heartbeat in her ears, but she couldn't win the fight against the sinking sensation taking over. Her head fell back against one muscled shoulder as he struggled to get them onto solid ice. "You're safe now."

"Where…is your…coat?" Her words slurred, her tongue too heavy in her mouth. Shouldn't he be wearing more clothes out here in the open? He was going to freeze to death. A low thumping filled her ears. Shea fought the exhaustion, the pain, the heaviness, but it was all too much.

"Don't worry about me. Help is coming. Focus on staying awake, you hear me?" Vincent increased the pressure around her middle. Sounds of dripping water overwhelmed the thumping in the distance as he slid her onto the ice, but she didn't have the energy to do anything more than close her eyes. Her body was shutting down, she knew that, but at least she wasn't alone this time. A hint of warmth bled into her face as Vincent framed her chin with one hand. "Shea, look at me. Open your eyes."

She wanted to. With every fiber of her being, she wanted to commit his face to memory. Wanted to thank him for saving her life. Wanted to tell him how working with him had given her a reason to keep going when she had nothing left to lose over these last few months. Putting the remnants of her strength into following orders, Shea narrowed on dark brown eyes tinted with a hint of green in the middle. She'd never noticed that before, the green. She'd spent so long trying to tamp down the way he made her feel when they were in the field together, she hadn't taken the time to really appreciate the man above her. But right now, her body was making the choice for her. She had all the time in the world. Water clung to his beard and hair, the tips already crusted with ice. His normally smooth, tanned skin had lost a bit of color, but the fire in his gaze pierced straight through her.

The pounding grew louder, vibrating up through her legs and into her chest. They'd taken down Grillo and his team—together—but the job wasn't done. Her attacker had contacts back in New York, people he'd ordered to surveil her ex-husband and her son. The organization that'd sent him, it was bigger than she and Vincent could've imagined, but she couldn't protect them anymore. "Find… Wells."

Vincent engulfed her hand in his, pressing the backs of her fingers to his mouth. "We're going to find him, Shea. Together. Just hang on."

The steady thumping pulsed at the base of her neck as rotors and a chopper's frame moved into her vision, but she couldn't win this war anymore.

"Shea," he said. "Shea!"

Chapter Nine

"You look like hell," a familiar voice said.

Vincent breathed through the relentless pain around two cracked ribs, a gunshot wound and the beginning of infection in his thigh, then focused on the woman beside the hospital bed. His stomach dropped. Not Shea. Although he wasn't disappointed to see Kate Monroe—the team's resident psychologist—hers wasn't the face he needed right now. Fluorescent lighting reflected off her blond-streaked hair pulled back in a low knot. She looked good, considering she and her thought-to-be-dead husband had barely survived a serial killer's hunt less than two months ago. Now here she was, her skin almost glowing, but maybe that was a side effect of the pregnancy. Vincent leveraged his weight into the mattress with his uninjured hand, careful of the new sling around his arm, and positioned himself higher in the bed. His head throbbed at the base of his skull, the lights too bright. "You say the nicest things, Doc." He couldn't stop the groan rumbling through his chest as he moved to throw off one of the hospital's heavy blankets. "Where's Shea?"

"Officer Ramsey is resting comfortably down the hall. The surgeon was able to retrieve the bullet in one piece without any complications. She'll make a full recovery as long as she gets the rest she needs. But knowing what I do about her, I don't see that happening anytime soon. That being the case, I'm having Braxton keep an eye on her." Kate crossed one leg over the other and sat back in the chair, that all-too-knowing gaze weighing on him. "You want to talk about what happened out there? About why you used Blackhawk resources to investigate a case, but didn't feel the need to involve the rest of your team?"

"Elizabeth." The network security analyst's name was torn from his mouth. He'd asked her to run the fingerprint he'd recovered from the warehouse fire that night through IAFIS. He should've known she'd push it up the ladder, but he couldn't blame her, either. Blackhawk's founder, Sullivan Bishop, required honesty from all his operatives. It wasn't fair of him to put that kind of pressure on one of his teammates. Or one of his closest friends.

"Give her credit." Kate crossed her arms and sat forward. "She didn't brief Sullivan about the fingerprint until after Search and Rescue recovered you and Shea on that lake. I think she was honestly more worried she'd missed something than anything else." Bright green eyes assessed him, as though she were trying to see inside his head. "We were all worried, Vincent. You've helped save every single one of your teammates' lives in the field. Did you really think we weren't going to do the same for you?"

Nausea replaced the focus of pain. "Everyone I've involved has paid the price, Kate. I've already lost two of my best investigators in New York, and I almost lost Shea out there." The thought spiked his blood pressure as acid climbed up his throat. This was on him. Everything—the plane crash, the bullet in her side, the fact that her son had been put in danger—it was all because of him. Her death would've been on his shoulders for the rest of his life. Just as IAB Officer Walter's would be. "I'm not going to risk the team."

"It's not over, is it? The people who shot you, whoever brought down your plane... They're still out there," Kate said. "They're not done with you or Officer Ramsey."

She was right. Shea had become as much a part of this as he had the moment he'd requested her as his partner on the joint investigations between Blackhawk and Anchorage PD. Had those bastards been watching her all this time? Watching her son and ex-husband in New York? If he'd known whoever'd killed IAB Officer Ashton Walter would come for her, Vincent would've stayed the hell away, kept her out of danger. "I can't tell you anything, Kate. Not without putting you and the baby, even Declan, at risk."

"We're a team, Vincent. You were there for me when the Hunter started closing in on Declan and me. You've been there for every single one of us. No matter the personal cost. Now it's time for us to be there for you." Her shoulders sank away from her ears with a hard exhale. Kate produced a pale manila folder, those inquisitive green eyes centered on the name written on the tab. Even from this distance, he read the label easily: Shea Ramsey. "When Blackhawk and Anchorage PD partnered on investigations a few months ago, I was asked to vet the officers who'd be working with us and get permission for the department to share their psych evals with me. Including Shea Ramsey."

Vincent sat a bit higher in the bed, the pain in his shoulder and thigh forgotten. "Don't do this, Kate."

"I can hear the difference in your voice when you talk about her, Vincent. I've seen the way you study her when you're working together." Kate ran her fingers over the edge of the folder. "I was there when the EMTs pushed you two through the emergency room doors. You were asking for her, even when your body was shutting down from diving into that lake. You're already falling for her, but she owes you the truth—"

"No, she doesn't." He bit back the anger in his voice as her head snapped up, shock evident in her expression. His pulse pounded hard behind his ears in perfect rhythm to the machines tracking his vitals, creating a tingling sensation beneath the skin of his face and neck. He understood the firm's need to vet the officers involved in their joint cases, but nothing—not a damn thing—would change his feelings for Shea. Anything important enough he needed to know about, she had the right to tell him herself. Not some department shrink who'd spent less than sixty minutes with her and come to some half-baked conclusion. Tugging the IV from the inner crease of his elbow, Vincent swung his legs over the bed. Over two hundred stitches, a mild concussion from being knocked unconscious, beginning stages of hypothermia…none of it mattered. He needed to see her. "I understand you're trying to look out for me, but this isn't the way to do it, Kate. Not only would I be betraying her privacy, but you're also putting yourself at risk by even thinking about telling me what's in that eval.

I know who Shea Ramsey is, and nothing in that file is going to convince me otherwise."

The profiler stood. Giving him room to maneuver to the end of the bed, she lowered her gaze to the floor, the file still clutched in her hand. "Even if it means she's not in a position to love you back?"

Vincent slowed. Cold worked up through his bare feet and deep into muscle. From the white tile floor or Kate's question, he had no idea and didn't care. Shea had stood by him when Grillo and his men had given her the chance to walk away. She'd prevented those bastards from throwing his body into the ranger station fire and given him something he'd lost a long time ago: hope. He wouldn't have made it this far without her, would've never discovered the truth about that night in the warehouse. She'd given him that, and so much more. Whether she realized it or not, he owed her his life. In more ways than one. Kate wasn't wrong. He'd started falling for Shea Ramsey a long time ago, and if she didn't feel the same way because of some deep-seated secret spelled out in that file... The pain in his ribs flared on a slow inhale. He wanted to hear it from her. "That's not your call to make."

"I don't want to see you get hurt," Kate said.

"You've seen the scars on my back, the stitches in my shoulder and the bruises on my ribs, Doc.

Seems all I've known lately is hurt." Stillness enveloped him as he thought back to that moment between him and Shea in the ranger station, before Grillo's men had burned the place to the ground. To the moment she'd blamed herself for her ex-husband cheating on her, for him filing for divorce and for the bastard taking her son from her. There were only a handful of reasons he could think of for a strong, determined woman like Shea not to fight back every step of the way, but for her to sever ties with her family and friends, for her to throw herself into her work more over the past few months than ever before, narrowed it considerably. Only one reason stood out from the rest, explained why she'd been able to show up for her city day after day as though nothing could break through that hardened exterior she was determined to hide behind despite the hardships going on in her personal life. And it'd all started after she'd given birth to Wells. Vincent met his teammate's gaze as understanding hit. He hadn't seen it until now, how much Shea had been suffering all this time. Afraid. Alone. How could he have been so blind? "Better than feeling nothing at all, right?"

"Right." Kate picked up a duffel from beside her chair he hadn't noticed until now and handed it to him. "Just be careful. With yourself, and with her."

He nodded. Vincent took the bag, waiting

for the profiler to leave before he dressed in the fresh set of clothes she'd brought, but he'd have to leave his boot laces untied on account of the bullet wound in his shoulder. He couldn't wait any longer. Wrenching open the door with his free hand, he headed down the hall, to the door where Braxton Levitt—Elizabeth Dawson's chosen partner and father of her child—stood armed and ready to protect Shea. Vincent acknowledged the former intelligence analyst, then knocked as Braxton stepped away from the door before pushing his way inside.

The breath rushed out of him as he caught sight of her at the end of the hospital bed. Long damp hair rested across her shoulders, revealing smooth hills of lean muscle along her back. He studied her wound beneath the bandage in nothing but a black lace bra and an unbuttoned pair of dirty jeans. Muscle and bruising. So much bruising his gut tightened. In an instant, fierce green eyes locked on him, and every cell in his body forgot the haziness of morphine he'd been under for the past few hours. She'd just gotten out of surgery. They both had. Now it looked like she was ready to run. "Where the hell do you think you're going?"

"I'm going to New York." Dropping her hands from the gauze taped at her side, she notched her chin level with the floor. "I'm going to get my son back."

Tension drained from him. Vincent tried crossing his arms over his chest, only to be reminded one of them was in a damn sling. She wanted to go to New York? Fine. He couldn't stop her, but he wasn't letting her get away that easily. Not after everything they'd survived together. "All right. When do we leave?"

"ANTHONY AND BENNETT have already made contact." Vincent maneuvered into his seat beside her, his clean, masculine scent overriding stale circulated air and body odor. He was trying to distract her. They'd taken off from Ted Stevens International Airport a few minutes ago, along with a hundred other passengers, and right now, she didn't want to focus on anything else other than him. Not the plane crash. Not the fact an organization of corrupt cops had gone after her son and nearly killed her in the process. And not about what her ex-husband would have to say the minute she showed her face at the safe house after he'd told her she'd never see Wells again unless she got herself help. "We'll be meeting your ex-husband, his wife and Wells in a secure location in two days to avoid tipping off Grillo's men. Until then, we'll hole up at one of Blackhawk's safe houses in Brooklyn."

"Two days." Anthony Harris, Blackhawk's weapons expert, and Bennett Spencer, the firm's

newest investigator Shea had never met, had both
volunteered for the job to protect her son. If Vincent trusted them to protect Wells until she could
reach him, then so did she, but her nerves still
hadn't settled. Had nothing to do with the chance
the plane would go down, or that she'd nearly died
in the exact same mountains they were flying over
right now. It was Vincent. No matter how many
times she'd tried, she couldn't reconcile the vigilante operative she'd known with the man who'd
risked his own life to dive into that lake and save
her. The man who'd fought off almost a dozen
armed corrupt cops to keep her safe. It'd been in
those last few moments, with Grillo's arm around
her throat as freezing lake water had seeped past
her lips, that'd she'd realized the truth. Vincent
wasn't who she'd believed. Not the secretive, in-
furiating know-it-all keen on breaking the rules
whenever he got the chance, but more. He'd detached himself from everyone around him in order
to protect them, kept them all in the dark about his
personal investigation, including his team, but he'd
trusted her. Why?

The plane jerked downward, and she couldn't
stop the flood of memories crashing through the
barrier she'd built as a distraction. The uncertainty,
the fear, the terrifying thought she'd never see her
son again. She closed her eyes against the inces-

sant shriek of the plane's engines, forced herself to breathe evenly as her heart threatened to beat out of her chest. It was just turbulence. She knew that, but—

Warmth enveloped her hand clutched around the shared armrest, and everything inside her stilled. The thudding at the back of her skull faded, nothing but her own breathing filling her ears as she opened her eyes. Her wet hair had dampened the back of her T-shirt after she'd showered back at the hospital, but that had nothing to with the sensations running down her spine now.

It was Vincent.

He'd pulled his hair back, exposing the fresh bruises along his jaw where Grillo had left his mark—bruises similar to hers—but none of it took away from the gut-wrenching intensity in his expression. Sensations simmered low in her abdominals the longer he studied her, and she suddenly found herself incapable of pretending he hadn't gotten to her these past few months. That he hadn't broken through the haze she'd been hiding behind for so long. The edges of where his tattoos met the scars on his back peeked out from beneath his T-shirt, and in that moment, she wanted nothing more than to trace the flesh with her fingertips. Just as she'd wanted to do back in that cave, buried under all that snow. His exhale tickled the oversensitized skin of her neck, and she couldn't fight back the shiver spreading across her shoulders.

"Careful, Freckles." His words practically vibrated through her, he was so close. "You keep looking at me like that and I might start to get ideas of finishing what we started back at the ranger station."

Heat surged through her. That kiss...it'd been everything she'd imagined and more between them. The desire, the rush of adrenaline, the familiarity despite the fact that they'd practically been strangers before getting on that plane. The backs of her knees tingled at the memory of his mountainous body pressed against hers, the feel of his heart beating hard beneath her palm. She'd done that to him. She'd spiked his pulse higher with desire, but with one kiss, he'd ripped her apart. Helped her remember who'd she'd been, and she never wanted to go back. Never wanted to be trapped in that lonely shell again. If anything, she wanted more. Because of him. What that meant for the future—if they had one—she didn't know, but the idea didn't seem impossible anymore. Not after everything they'd been through. His eyes glittered with brightness as though he could see the battle wreaking havoc inside her. "Thank you for what you did. For...getting me out of the plane, for sharing the food your mom packed, even when it meant you'd starve if I didn't make it."

"Oh, don't worry, she packed more." Vincent released her hand and hauled his bag from between his feet, showing her the row of food containers inside.

"I'll be sure to thank her." A laugh burst from her chest, resurrecting the agony in her side. She couldn't remember the last time she'd let go like this, but the hollowness in her chest still hurt, and her laugh died in a renewed drone from the plane's engines. She set the crown of her head back against the headrest. Flittering her fingers over his forearm, Shea noted the rise of goose bumps across his skin where she touched him.

"I haven't felt like myself for a long time now, but you…" She forced a smile, the pressure of unshed tears building. The swirl of brown in his eyes warmed her straight to her core, drowning the uncertainty clawing through her. He deserved to know the truth after what he'd done for her, deserved to know that her path to healing wasn't over, that anything that happened between them might not end the way they imagined. Not right now. But she would always be grateful for him demanding to be her partner, even if he and his team believed they were above the law. She breathed in his light hint of soap, held on to it as long as she could. Would he still view her as that strong, determined, independent woman he'd described back at the ranger station when he learned the truth? Would he still want to partner with her when all of this was over? Dread pooled in her stomach. Would he still trust her?

"Shea?" he asked.

Shea removed her hand from his arm. Her ex-husband hadn't understood why there were days when she hadn't been able to get out of bed, hadn't been able to make love to him or to take care of Wells. Why she'd thrown herself into her work to the point she couldn't keep the details of her cases straight from working double and triple shifts straight through. Tears prickled at her lower lash line, but she held on to them. The answer was clear. Nobody could understand the mental war she fought to stay present every day. Not even Vincent. "Working with you these past few months saved me. Thank you."

"You would've saved yourself sooner or later." He maneuvered the duffel back onto the floor between his feet, the pain in his ribs evident as his expression contorted. He'd taken two bullets to the chest for her. If it weren't for the Kevlar vest he'd retrieved from one of Grillo's men, she wouldn't have made it back to the surface of the lake. She owed him her life, and she'd do whatever it took to pay him back. "I was just there to get the crap kicked out of me."

"Oh, *that's* why you were following me down the mountain. It all makes sense now." Stinging shot through her mouth as she forced another smile, and she set her hand against her lips. They'd fought off the men sent to kill them two days ago, but the pain of her injuries hadn't lessened. "For what it's worth, I wouldn't be here if it weren't for you."

"Guess that makes us even." He leaned back in his seat, closing his eyes. Couldn't blame him. He hadn't gotten a whole lot of rest before she'd checked herself out of the hospital to get on the next flight to New York. Neither of them had, but she wasn't going to sit around and wait for whoever'd sent Grillo and his men to take another run at her son. She'd already failed Wells once. She wouldn't fail him again. "Blackhawk would be looking for my toasty remains if you hadn't shot that bastard."

"Right." A minute passed, maybe two. The flight attendant's voice from the front of the plane fought to keep her in the present, but Shea only had attention for him. The way his dark lashes rested on his cheeks, how a set of stitches from his fight with Grillo slashed down through one naturally arched eyebrow. She couldn't help but memorize every detail, every imperfection, every ridge and valley of muscle exposed in the light of the plane's dim lighting. All too easily, she envisioned the woman lucky.enough to have him all to herself. He was a warrior and a hell of an investigator. He'd protect his life partner until his last breath, just as he'd protected her after the crash, and a knot of jealousy formed behind her sternum. What would it be like to be his? She followed the curve of his neck to the point where his tattoos climbed to the base of his skull.

"You still want to touch them, don't you?" he asked.

How had he known? The pressure of his attention gave her pause, and a prickling sensation spread into her face. She didn't know what to say, didn't know how to explain the compulsion to touch him. Not the Blackhawk Security investigator he presented to the world but the man he'd been before that, the one he kept hidden under sarcastic remarks, secrets and banter. She wanted to touch the cop who'd almost died in a fire in the middle of a crime scene so he could find the truth.

His seat protested over the high-pitched drone of the engines as he shifted forward, close, so close. Dark brown eyes steadied on her, and the hairs on the back of her neck stood on end. "All right, Freckles, as soon as we're safe, I'm all yours."

Chapter Ten

He'd meant every word on the plane.

Shouldering his duffel up the eight stairs off Herkimer Street, Vincent hit the four-digit code into the keypad beside the large black double doors leading into the safe house and motioned Shea inside. Instincts on alert, he scanned down both ends of the street. Her fresh scent chased back the smell of recycled air, diesel and humidity as she maneuvered past him, but he couldn't pay it much attention now that they'd finally made it to New York. Grillo was dead, but that didn't mean he and Shea hadn't been flagged by the rest of his organization when they'd landed. The brownstone Blackhawk's founder and CEO had secured them for the next two days had to have cost the firm well over Vincent's yearly salary, but in this situation, no amount of money was too much to keep his partner safe.

Windows positioned only at the front and the

back of the property, military-grade security system installed by Blackhawk specialists, closed-circuit surveillance at the front and back doors recording every car that passed, every face that came within ten feet of the door. The place was located less than ten blocks from the safe house Anthony Harris and Bennett Spencer had secured for Shea's son. He'd made her a promise, and Vincent didn't intend to back down. He'd get her to Wells.

She slid her backpack—the same one that'd saved their lives in the wilderness—from her shoulder, but still clutched the worn strap as she studied the house. The front entryway led into a massive living room with pale hardwood floors and an extravagant old fireplace repainted white, with the entire upper half of the wall made of worn red brick. Gold-and-white art had been hung on either side of the fireplace, attempting to bring the hundred-year-old building into this decade, but there was a physical history to these houses. Vincent heard it in the way the floor creaked as Shea moved toward the turquoise couch positioned at one end of the living room, saw the dust that'd built up on the higher rows of bricks along the wall. Sunlight pierced the floor-to-ceiling glass doors at the back of the house, just beyond the modern white kitchen, making the green of her eyes somehow brighter. In that moment, the bruises faded, the color in her cheeks returned, and shadows under her eyes disappeared. She made broken look beautiful, and he couldn't look away. "This is a safe house?"

He nodded toward the alarm panel set behind him off one side of the entry doors. "We did the security work for the owner a few months ago. When I briefed the team about the case, Sullivan reached out to see if he'd be willing to let us rent the house for a couple days. Guess they came to an arrangement."

"It's beautiful." She skimmed long fingers over the railing of the banister leading up to the second floor. Notching her chin over one shoulder, she refused to meet his gaze. "And the security system—"

"We'll be safe here." He'd make sure of it. Vincent closed the small space between them, his boots echoing from the combination of hardwood flooring and the open concept architecture of the home. He dropped the duffel at his feet. Sliding his hand to her hips, he tugged her into his chest. Stress corded the tendons between her neck and shoulder as he traced his mouth along the outside of her ear, and she relaxed back into him. Ebbing pain spread from the bruises where he'd taken two to the chest, but he'd choose the discomfort over ending up six feet under. Pain had become his friend after the fire, his ally. It told him he wasn't dead yet. "I gave you my word, Shea. I'm not going to let anything happen to you or your son. I'm going to end this."

"No." She turned in his arms, her tired gaze locked on his. Dark hair fell in curls around her face, and he ached to run his hands through the strands to confirm they were as soft as he remembered. "We're in this together, remember? A team. Survive together or die alone."

"This isn't your fight." Grillo and his men had nearly killed her. He couldn't stand the thought of putting her life—her son's life—at risk again because he hadn't been careful enough, but letting her walk away, move on with her life… Vincent breathed in her sultry scent, held on to it, made it part of him, then let it go. He'd walk away to keep her safe, to help her get her life back. No matter what'd happened in the past or what that damn psych evaluation said, she deserved to be happy. With or without him. He spread his free hand over her arm, locking down the flood of desire rushing through him. "Elizabeth can get you and your son new identities. You could go anywhere you wanted, get as far away from this nightmare as possible. You'd be safe. They'd never be able to find you."

For her protection, neither would he.

Shea lowered her chin, and his heart jerked in his chest. Would she take him up on his offer? Would she disappear from his life? Reaching out, she intertwined her fingers with his, then looked up at him through long dark lashes. She pulled him toward the stairs leading to the second floor, her hair falling in waves over her back. Nervous energy pulsed down his spine as they climbed each stair, then exploded as she led them into the first bedroom on the second floor. The same pale hardwood ran along the length of the room with another wall of deep red brick wrapping one wall. The fireplace, similarly painted as the one downstairs, demanded attention near the queen-size bed, but Vincent only had awareness for her, for the hesitation in her expression as she faced him in the center of the big room. Her lips parted, her tongue swiping between them, and his insides jumped. "I'm safe with you."

Angling her head up, she stepped into him, fingers fisted into his T-shirt as she rose on her toes to reach him. Her soft mouth smoothed over his slowly, unsure, but after a few moments worked to claim every part of him. Faster, deeper, desperate. Her fingernails bit into the back of his neck, searing his skin, as though she intended to make them one, but he didn't pull away. Hints of mint toothpaste teased his senses, and goose bumps rose on the back of his neck. Hell, he couldn't get enough of her. She tasted of strength, stubbornness and vulnerability, and she was hiking his blood pressure higher with each stroke of her tongue against his. The bullet wound in his shoulder protested as he leveraged his free hand under her rib cage and lifted her against him.

She wrapped those powerful legs around his waist, easing the pressure in his arms, but he didn't give a damn about the pain. There was only her. Threading her fingers through his hair, she broke the kiss as he pressed her back against the brick wall surrounding the ornate fireplace. Her unsteady exhale skidded across his neck as she framed his jaw with one hand. Desire swirled in the jade-green depths of her eyes. "I'm glad you're here."

"Me, too." He toed off his boots, still holding on to her as best he could. Because there was no way in hell he was letting her go. Not now. Not ever. Stitches pulled tight in his right thigh, but there wasn't a damn thing that was going to stop him from memorizing every inch of her body. "Otherwise I might not be able to get this sling off myself."

"I can help with that." The sensual promise in her voice hit him square in the gut. With a brilliant smile, she straightened her legs, sliding along the length of him until she hit the floor.

She worked her fingers under the straps of his sling, and within seconds, he was hauling the material and his T-shirt over his head. Her eyes widened as she took in the damage from the two bullets he'd caught in the vest, the bloodied gauze taped to his shoulder. But before he had the chance to tell her it was okay, that they didn't have to do this, her hands were on him. Heat tunneled down through his skin, into muscle, as she traced the patterns across his chest. "I don't want to hurt you."

Even if it means she's not in a position to love you back? Kate's words echoed through his mind. The truth was, Shea could hurt him. Worse than any fire, any bullet and any piece of shrapnel, but for the first time since Sullivan Bishop had found him in that warehouse with second- and third-degree burns over 30 percent of his back, Vincent was willing to take the risk. He didn't give a damn what some department shrink had written in her psych eval. They didn't know Shea like he did. He caught her hand in his, brought the tips of her fingers to his mouth. The lie came easily enough. "You couldn't ever hurt me, Freckles."

"What makes you so sure?" she asked.

He slid his hand into the waterfall of hair above her ear. Hell, it was just as soft as before, maybe even more so, but he saw past that beauty to the steel underneath, to the woman who'd risked her life for a chance to save his, the woman who'd suffered so much, yet kept putting others' needs ahead of her own. "Because you protect people. I know you'd never hurt anyone if you could help it. Not even me."

He offered her his hand, as she had downstairs, and maneuvered her through the bathroom door to their left. He hit the light, out of patience to notice anything other than the wall of glass housing a large open shower. In seconds, he twisted the rain shower head on and stripped them both bare as steam filled the space, being careful of her wound. Leading her beneath the spray, Vincent reveled in the feel of her skin against his. Hot water seared his skull and seeped into his wounds, but it was nothing compared to the sensations her hands generated as she traced the pattern of scars on his back. He claimed her mouth again, sweeping his tongue past the seam of her lips, memorizing her, making her part of him. Making them one.

SHE HADN'T BEEN intimate with anyone since her divorce. Not until Vincent.

She could still smell him on her, the hint of soap and man that somehow had been driven deep into her pores. Shea shifted in the passenger seat of the rental SUV as the memories of those delirium-inducing hours played across her mind. After their shower, they'd managed to make it to the bed, and she'd lost herself in him, in pleasure, in escape, to the point she hadn't been able to tell her fantasies from reality. There'd only been him. He'd been all male, full of power he barely contained as he'd pushed her entire body into overdrive. His touch had awakened feelings and sensations she'd lost to the darkness of her depression. Within just a few hours, everything had returned to full color.

They'd talked, laughed, learned about each other. She'd listened as he recounted the night of the fire, how Blackhawk's founder had found him barely breathing and gotten him the help he'd needed. How Sullivan Bishop had recruited him to the firm and promised to help Vincent find the people who'd lit the match. She'd opened up about her brother's death, how she'd become a cop to keep the blood running blue in her family. How she'd crossed oceans for people her entire life who hadn't ever considered crossing a bridge for her, people like her ex. She'd drifted off to sleep sometime in the afternoon, wrapped in his arms. Wrapped in safety. Shea cut her gaze to him in the driver's seat, her breathing steady despite the pain in her side. She hadn't felt that kind of peace in a long time.

Now they were parked outside the warehouse where it'd all begun. The murder scene of IAB Officer Ashton Walter and the two technicians Vincent had lost the night of the fire remained eerily quiet, nothing but her rhythmic pulse soft at the base of her throat. Dim street lighting revealed graffiti painted across boarded windows and doors. A strip of yellow crime scene tape lifted from the pavement in front of one of the rolltop doors with the breeze. Burn patterns darkened the perimeter of the second-floor windows at one end of the warehouse, and her insides clenched. All too easily, she imagined Vincent at the center of an entire building threatening to come down on him at any moment, the flames closing in, the pain. All because he'd been doing his job. If it hadn't been for the man who'd become his boss, would Vincent have made it out alive? She didn't want to think about the answer.

"No movement." Nothing to suggest they were walking into an ambush, but they weren't going to move into position until they were absolutely sure Grillo's organization hadn't been doing their own surveillance. Sliding her hand over his, she studied his hardened expression. "Are you sure you want to do this?"

"I have to. It's the only way to uncover the truth." In her next breath, he reached into the back seat for the pair of bolt cutters and a borrowed forensic case and shouldered out of the SUV. He hit the pavement, and she followed close on his heels.

Shea scanned both ends of the street lined with warehouses, parked cars and strobing fluorescent lighting from worn signage. The district played host to a variety of industries, mostly industrial with lots stretching as far back as the East River like this one. Easier access for deliveries from the docks. Jogging across the street, she followed him to the east side of the building and pressed her back against the cinder blocks while he cut through a padlock located beneath the warning sticker NYPD had sealed against the door. Her instincts told her they should've looped in local authorities, but then again, the men who'd attacked her and Vincent in the mountains had been local authorities. They couldn't trust the police. And if she couldn't trust the very people who were supposed to protect innocent lives, she didn't know who to trust anymore. Except Vincent.

"Got it." The door hinged inward, nothing but darkness and the scent of burnt toast and gasoline on the other side. With a glance toward her, he nodded once before his mountainous outline disappeared inside.

Shea retrieved the flashlight from her jacket and brought the beam to life before unholstering the weapon Vincent had given her back at the safe house. The hairs on the back of her neck stood on end as she shuffled through debris, broken glass and puddles of rain water that'd come through the leaking roof. The small amount of research she'd done on that night reported it'd taken NYFD close to six hours to extinguish the fire. An accelerant had been used, officials narrowing it down to gasoline, which explained the slight burn in her nostrils. She tried breathing through her mouth, focusing on Vincent's outline, and pushed ahead to a cleared section of ashes. Dread collected in the pit of her stomach. Every inch of the floor had been covered in debris, except for the two body-sized areas here. Was this where EMTs had found Vincent's team?

"Over here." His voice echoed off what was left of the aluminum roofing, intense, isolated, and warning slid up her spine.

She found him crouched over a similar cleared section of ash, her beam highlighting the tension in the muscles down his back. Winter in New York City wasn't quite as frigid as Anchorage, but the cold still worked through her clothing and into her bones. Her breath solidified into crystalized puffs in front of her mouth as she redirected the flashlight beam to the floor—and froze. "That's a bullet casing." Warped from the looks of it. At least old enough to blend into the landscape of ash, dried blood and dirt. She wouldn't have recognized the casing for what it was unless she'd been looking in that exact spot for evidence. She scanned the area around the casing but couldn't see more than a few feet in circumference. "Hard to believe the techs or the fire department managed to miss something like that after the fire. They would've had investigators all over this place."

"Without having access to my lab, my guess is the casing is about the same age as the fire. This one is nearly melted into the floor." The sound of plastic over gravel shot her heart into her throat as he slid his forensic case closer and popped the lock. He snapped latex gloves over his hands and peeled an evidence bag from the roll in his kit. Carefully, he collected the casing from the floor and dropped it into the bag, and she couldn't help but watch every move he made. This was what he'd been trained for. He was in his element here, intense, focused, alert, and she couldn't help but admire his attention to detail. "But the casing over there is newer." Vincent redirected his flashlight a few feet from where he crouched, highlighting the metallic shell. "Both were shot from a .38 Smith & Wesson. Same caliber the medical examiner recovered from Ashton Walter's body."

Two casings. Two different time lines. "You

think the people who killed that IAB officer might've kept using this location to carry out their executions?" On one hand, that theory made sense. FDNY and NYPD had condemned the building after the fire, making it impossible for another business to occupy the space, which gave an organization of corrupt cops the exact opportunity they needed to carry on with business as usual. On the other hand, using the same location where they'd committed their previous crimes could be considered careless. "I don't see a man like Grillo leaving evidence behind for us to find."

"No." He studied the first casing in the glow of his flashlight. "In my experience, cops make the best criminals." Shifting his gaze to her, he straightened and pocketed the evidence bag. He directed his flashlight to the second piece of evidence. "They know how to clean up after themselves, which means someone could've left this beauty behind on purpose, or the shooter has gotten too comfortable with their overloaded sense of power and figured no one would be able to connect the evidence to them if it was recovered."

Warning screamed through her.

"But Grillo knew you hadn't dropped the case. He knew you'd come back to this scene if he didn't stop you." Shea spun on her heel and swung her weapon high as movement registered from the door they'd broken through. She backed up a few steps, instinctively maneuvering herself in front of Vincent. Her shoulder brushed against his arm, and she lowered her voice. "The casing could be a distraction to keep us here."

"It's a trap." Vincent wrapped his uninjured hand around her arm and tugged her back. Her foot collided with a metal bracket, the scrape of steel and concrete loud in her ears. Exactly what the people who'd followed them would need to locate them. Staticed voices echoed through the shadows. "Follow me. Stay low and use me as a shield if you have to."

"We can't leave the other casing here. It's evidence." She reached for the shell.

Vincent pulled her into his chest and shoved her forward before she had a chance to collect the evidence. "We don't have time."

She switched off her flashlight to conceal their position, gripping the gun in her hand tighter. Before her eyes had a chance to adjust, Vincent was pulling her deeper into the warehouse, her hand enveloped in his. Shouts pierced the sound of her shallow breathing, then a gunshot overhead. She ducked low while trying to keep pace with Vincent, heart in her throat as they ran through the maze of debris and structural damage. How could've Grillo's organization known they were here?

Glass shattered to her right a split second before a bright burst of light and an ear-piercing boom threw her off her balance, but Vincent fought to keep her upright and moving. "I've got you. Just keep going."

Smoke filled her lungs as they raced to the back of the property. There were more flashes, more explosions from behind. The muscles in her legs burned. They couldn't go back to the SUV. If the same people who'd sent Grillo had been surveilling the building all this time, there was a chance they'd already flagged the plates and were waiting to follow her and Vincent back to the safe house. They couldn't risk it. They'd have to escape on foot.

Vincent released her hand, then lowered his uninjured shoulder as he rammed into the only door at the back of the warehouse. But it wouldn't budge. He tried again. Nothing.

The door had to have been padlocked, like the one they'd come through at the front. The voices were getting closer, the smoke from the stun grenades thinning. Shea raised her weapon, bracing one leg slightly behind her as she'd been trained, her weight on the balls of her feet. The windows back here were boarded, nothing but burnt cinder blocks surrounding them. There was nowhere else to go, and she wasn't sure she had enough rounds to take on another team of corrupt cops. Her breath rushed out of her. "Vincent…"

The door swung open, and Shea twisted around to follow him out. Only someone was blocking the door. Two shots. Three. The bullets ripped past her left arm almost in slow motion before embedding into two gunmen who'd broken through the layer of smoke. They both went down, and Shea turned to confront the woman with the gun.

"Hello, Vincent." Long blonde hair draped over the woman's shoulder as she lowered her weapon to reveal a stark face and bright blue eyes. "I told you this case would get you killed."

Chapter Eleven

"Officer Shea Ramsey, Anchorage PD, meet Lieutenant Lara Richards, my former commanding officer." The last person he'd ever expected to see. Vincent pressed his back against the cold countertop in the kitchen of their safe house. They'd barely made it out of the warehouse alive. Wouldn't have if it weren't for Lara, but he didn't believe in coincidence. Grillo's people hadn't been the only ones watching that location.

"Nice to meet you." Shea stretched out her hand with a nod, shook Lara's hand and stepped back. "Not sure we would've gotten out of the building if it weren't for you."

Lara's bright blue gaze studied Shea. At well over five foot ten, with lengthy, model-like features, perfectly straight teeth and lithe movements, Lara Richards had done their forensics unit proud for the nine years she'd been his commanding officer. With her help, his team had an 85 percent closure rate. They'd closed so many cases—new and cold—she was being considered for a captain's position at the Eleventh at the time he'd left the squad. Vincent had even considered taking her job once she made the move. Until she'd shut down his theory IAB Officer Ashton Walter's murderer had come from law enforcement. She'd warned him to drop the case, said his personal investigation into who shot Officer Walter would get him killed. She hadn't been wrong. After the fire, Sullivan Bishop had gotten him out of town so fast, he didn't have the chance to prove his theory to her. Now here she stood. "Can't say I was there by coincidence. I've been watching one of the officers who was at the warehouse tonight for the past few months. Ever since I heard about what happened to Vincent here the night of the fire." Lara turned her attention back to him. "You're lucky to be alive."

Wasn't the first time someone had said those words to him. "What are you doing here, Lara?"

"For starters, I wanted to apologize. I should've listened when you originally came to me about the four unsolved homicides over a year ago. If I had, maybe I wouldn't have lost three of my best investigators that night." She pulled her shoulders back, the lighting from overhead shifting across her leather jacket. She lowered her chin toward her chest, eyes downcast to the purse she'd set on the counter. Pulling a tablet from within, she swiped her fingers across the screen, then handed it to him. "But maybe I can make up for that now."

"What's this?" He scanned the documents on the screen. Case files. The four files he'd been assigned to investigate. Shea stepped into his side, her light scent in his lungs, and just like that, he fell into the memories of her body wrapped around his between the sheets. She'd trusted him for those short few hours, given him a part of herself she hadn't given to anyone since her divorce. He'd never forget that, never forget the glimpse of unfiltered happiness he'd witnessed as they memorized every inch of each other's bodies. He'd never seen anything more beautiful than when she'd smiled at him afterward. His back tingled in remembrance, the feel of her nails tracing patterns across his scars fresh. Unlike the other women he'd been with, she hadn't turned away from him in disgust or refused to look at the damage. If anything, she'd been drawn to it, as though she understood the physical and mental pain he carried.

"After you disappeared, I went back through your files and dug these out of cold cases. In your notes, you'd reported all four scenes had been cleaned by a professional, maybe someone in law enforcement or with forensic training." Lara crossed her arms over her chest, sinking in on herself as she leaned against the countertop. "You couldn't find any connection between the victims other than the first two, an investigative reporter for a local paper and her assistant." Her heels clicked on the tile as she rounded the island, and she swiped her finger across the tablet's screen in his hand. "The third victim was a public defender, and the last a rookie barely out of the academy more than two months. All four victims were shot with a .38 caliber, matching most of the NYPD's service weapons, and I think they were all killed for trying to uncover the truth."

"That's the same caliber of the casing we recovered from the warehouse," Shea said. "So you know there's a group of corrupt cops growing within the NYPD?"

"Yes." The weight of Lara's gaze pinned him in place, and she swiped her finger across the screen once more. "And I have proof. Like I said, I've been following one of the men from the warehouse for a few months now. I was able to clone his phone to see who he's been contacting, surveil his email, access his photos, everything. It seems the NYPD is aware of the group's existence and what they've been doing, but it's impossible to identify members of the organization or bring charges against them without raising suspicion. Any threat to the organization, like these four victims, is dealt with in-house. And they're good at what they do."

Vincent understood that better than most. "Brass has to be involved then. There's no way an entity like this could cover their asses so thoroughly unless they had upper management running the show."

"You might be right," Lara said.

"What have you been able to recover from the officer you're following?" Shea took the tablet, long fingers scrolling through the evidence his former commanding officer had gathered. "Anything we can use to expose the organization and what they've been doing?"

Lara straightened. "As far as I can tell, he's low on the totem pole, more like an errand boy. He and a partner hit up small-business owners for protection money, deliver and collect shipments, surveil and photograph targets. Guys like this follow orders, even the ones that involve executions like your four victims here." She stopped Shea from swiping to the next screen. "And those orders? They're all coming from one source. Officer Charlie Grillo."

Shea's soft exhale filled his ears, and it took everything in him not to bring her into his arms. Looking at the face of the man who'd threatened to kill her son, who'd almost killed her, was bound to cause a reaction, but now wasn't the time to forget why they'd come to New York in the first place. "Grillo came after us in Alaska. He brought down our plane, tried to kill us because Vincent ran the fingerprint he recovered from the death scene of that IAB officer through IAFIS. Ashton Walter."

"You think Walter was another victim who got too close?" Lara asked.

"I went to IAB after you refused to run my theory up the chain of command, and Grillo's people killed him for it. Then the bastards tried to kill me." Dread pooled at the bottom of his stomach as he studied the SOB's service record. Vincent had seen the original homicide crime scene photos before, but now, knowing who might be behind the killings, his blood pressure spiked higher. He could've stopped this, could've done something to keep these dirty cops from endangering innocent lives sooner. Like their pilot, like Shea and her family, his team. Vincent tried to keep the emotion out of his voice. It'd be easy to pin everything that'd happened up until now on Officer Charlie Grillo. There was just one problem. "Grillo was a beat cop. Hard to believe he had the power to keep an entire organization in line on his own, let alone convince his superiors to look the other way. Someone else—someone with a lot more authority—has to be pulling the strings now that Grillo's dead."

"If there is, I haven't been able to prove it." Lara shifted her weight between both feet, her expression never changing. "The two men who came after you tonight have been sitting on that building for a while. My guess is they were waiting for you. There's a chance they don't know their boss is dead yet. Could've just been following orders."

Or the real head of the organization was waiting to finish the job Grillo had started.

"You said you recovered a casing from the warehouse where I found you?" Lara asked.

"Haven't gotten the chance to run testing on it yet, but it could be exactly what we need to bring these bastards down." Vincent wrapped his hand around the warped bullet casing recovered from the warehouse inside his jacket pocket. He'd left his forensic kit back at the scene once the bullets started flying, along with the second piece of evidence, but his instincts said this casing was more important than being simply used as a distraction. He needed to get it analyzed. "But without access to the NYPD's labs, I'll need my team to run the tests, and that's only going to put the rest of them in danger."

"I can get you access," Lara said.

Shea's sharp gasp hiked his pulse higher, and

she closed the distance between herself and the counter, shoving the tablet at Lara, and every cell in his body woke with battle-ready tension. "This photo... Where did you get this photo?"

"I don't..." His former commanding officer's mouth parted slightly, obviously taken aback by Shea's panic. "I don't know. Maybe from the officer's phone I've been surveilling. I didn't see how it was relevant to the case, so I... I buried it in the back of the file until I had more time to identify the subjects."

Vincent spun the tablet toward him. The photo had been taken with a phone, nothing fancy, but clear enough for him to recognize Anthony Harris, Bennett Spencer, Logan Ramsey, Logan's new wife and Shea's son. Wells. "We can identify them." He shifted his attention to Shea, watched the color drain from her face. She stumbled back a few steps, but he caught her in time before she hit the opposite counter. Bringing her into his side for stability, he leveled his attention on Lara. "The location, too."

Damn it. The second safe house had been compromised. Shea's family was still in danger. He tapped the information button on the screen to check the time the surveillance photo had been taken, but it didn't look like the image had originated from the officer's phone. It'd been sent to him. Three hours ago. Right as he and Shea had arrived on scene at the warehouse. Gravity pulled at him. Shea had been right. Grillo's people had been counting on him to return to the warehouse, left the fresh bullet casing as a distraction to keep them occupied. So the bastards could follow through with their threat.

"Call them." Shea's voice shook as she stared up at him. "Now."

"What's going on?" Lara studied the photo, confusion evident in her expression. "Who are these people?"

Vincent didn't answer, punching in Anthony's cell number, and brought the phone to his ear. One ring. Two. Before voice mail. Desperation climbed across his chest, into his wound. He dialed Bennett's phone next.

No answer.

THE FOG WAS BACK.

Her pulse thudded loud behind her ears, the floor pulling at every muscle she owned. Everything seemed to move in slow motion. Three hours. Three hours since they'd gotten confirmation the safe house where Wells had been secured had been raided. Three hours her son had been out there, alone, in the hands of killers.

Blackhawk operatives moved around the house,

relaying orders, taking both Logan's and his new wife's statements as they patched head lacerations and checked their cognitive reflexes, more men and women trying to get a location for her son. Light from a laptop screen illuminated Elizabeth Dawson's face as she reviewed hours upon hours of traffic camera footage. Elliot Dunham, Blackhawk's private investigator, had never looked more serious than he did right then huddled over Elizabeth's shoulder. Sullivan Bishop checked and inventoried weapons as he barked orders at the rest of his team. Even Kate Monroe, the psychologist, had caught the next plane to New York, her green gaze steady on Shea, but she wasn't in the mood to talk about her feelings, about what was going through her head. She wanted her son back. Anthony Harris, the operative assigned to protect Wells, was still missing, along with Bennett Spencer. The entire Blackhawk Security team had rallied with a single call from Vincent.

Shea didn't recognize the other agents. Didn't care. The safe house had been secure. How had Grillo's organization found her son? Her ears rang, and she pressed the tips of her fingers to her temples in an attempt to drown out the horde of bees buzzing in her head. Wells was supposed to be safe.

"Shea." Vincent crouched in front of her. His

warm hands slid up her thighs for balance, but she couldn't focus on him. Not even with him this close. "I need to know what's going through your head right now."

"I should've been there." The words left her mouth without any inflection, a mere ghost of the numbness clawing through her insides, and she winced against the effect. Sliding her gaze to his, she felt as though she were standing on the edge of the cliff. All it would take was one tug, one slip, and she'd lose everything all over again. "I should've protected him."

He shook his head as though to tell her there was nothing she could've done. "We had two of our best operatives assigned to protect him—"

"Then how the hell did this happen?" Anger exploded through her, sharp, hot and unfiltered. Shea pushed to her feet, forcing him to back up a few steps, and slammed her hands against his chest. Then again. Heat seared from her scalp down to her toes, and she gave in to it because it was better than feeling nothing at all. "How did they get to my son, Vincent? I want to know!"

He didn't answer. Only took everything she had to give and more, absorbing each hit as tears burned in her eyes. Wrapping his arms around her, he fought to contain her, to comfort her, but it wasn't any use. She'd failed her son. Again.

Vincent tugged her into his chest as the sobs tore through her until she stilled, her ear pressed against his heart. He tangled his hands down through her hair, his cheek pressing against the crown of her head. "Whoever's behind this—whoever sent Grillo—they're trained just as well as we are, they're armed, and they've already proven the law doesn't apply to them." Silence descended in the house, but she didn't dare open her eyes, didn't want to see how many people were watching them. "But I told you Blackhawk protects their own, no matter what it takes, and we're going to get your son back."

She forced her eyes open, nails biting into his chest.

Every single operative in the room stood around them, frozen. Then the ice she'd felt for the team she'd resented for so long started to melt. Elizabeth stood up from her laptop and nodded. Elliot Dunham half saluted with that sarcastic grin she'd come to hate over the course of the past two years. Vincent's former commanding officer took position beside Elizabeth, and Kate Monroe smiled as Sullivan Bishop approached with a gun in his hand. Sea-blue eyes steadied on her. "When someone attacks one of us, they attack all of us, Officer Ramsey. And we're not going to let them get away with it. You're not alone in this fight." He studied the team behind him, then turned back to her. "You never will be again."

A fresh wave of tears threatened to fall, but Shea forced herself to straighten, to wipe the back of her hand across her face. To do what it'd taken her so long to do the first time: accept help. With the entire Blackhawk Security team on her side, the last people she ever would've asked for help, her confidence grew. They were going to get her son back. "Thank you."

"I want a location on Anthony and Bennett in the next minute, Liz, or I'm going to partner you with Elliot to hunt them down on foot." Another nod from Sullivan ended the conversation, and his agents got back to work. He shifted his attention to Vincent. "Get this woman a gun."

The buzz in her head died as Vincent pulled a weapon from his lower back and offered it to her, but she didn't dare meet his gaze when her fingers brushed his. He'd always viewed her as a strong, driven, independent woman, but her weakness had just rushed front and center for everyone to see. She cleared her throat as she checked the weapon. "Did Logan and his wife say anything that will give us a lead on who took Wells? Or how Grillo's organization found him in the first place?"

"Last thing Anthony reported back was his intention to move your family to another location because he'd spotted the same man walking past the safe house three times within a couple hours. From what Logan and his wife stated, Anthony left the safe house after telling them to lock the doors behind him, and that's when the explosion happened. A car bomb right outside the building. It happened so fast, Bennett hadn't been able to enable the security system before they breached the safe house." His hand remained on her lower back, steadying, comforting, but nothing could chase back the fear boiling under her skin. "With Anthony out of the way, he wasn't able to hold off the four-man team as they went for Wells. They were outnumbered and outgunned."

She couldn't breathe. Couldn't think. Shea closed her eyes against the images in her head, her fingernails biting into the center of her palms. Setting her forehead against his chest, she listened to the beat of his heart in an attempt to escape the desperation spreading through her. Fire and police were on scene at the safe house, but without the location of her son, there was nothing they could do. "And there hasn't been any contact from the team that took him."

"No, but…" Vincent's hesitation took on physical form when he didn't elaborate.

The tension only increased as she looked up at him. Living through the numbness over the past year had been the worst experience of her life. She didn't want to fall back into that cloud of darkness. She wanted to be there for her son, to be the mother he deserved, to feel like the woman Vincent believed her to be. But if she lost Wells…

"But what?"

"I need you to understand something, Shea. Anthony and Bennett are two of the best-trained operatives we have. Both served in the military and never would've given up Wells easily, even under torture. Anthony's got a kid of his own and one on the way, and Bennett risked everything to find his sister when she went missing." Pressure built in her chest the longer he stared down at her. "The only way they would've backed down was if the gunmen threatened to hurt your son."

She pulled back as the truth hit. "They're using Wells to draw me out."

"You're not just a loose end anymore, Shea." His uninjured hand slid along her forearms, eliciting goose bumps along the way. "Whoever's behind this is targeting you because they know how I feel about you, and they will use any means necessary to take me out."

The breath rushed out of her, heat flaring in her face. "How you feel about me?"

He closed the small distance between them.

"I lost everything that night. After I recovered

from the burns, I couldn't trust anyone with what I knew for fear it'd put their lives in danger, which only isolated me more from the people around me, including my team. I was at the point of giving up on this investigation, of living with this guilt for the rest of my life because there was nothing else I could do. Not without risking more innocent lives." Vincent wrapped her hand in his. "Until I met you. You're the reason I want to solve this case, Shea. Working with you these past few months, getting to know the woman who wouldn't back down from any challenge in her way, gave me the push I needed to see this through. Because if I don't solve this case, I don't have a future. And I want a future, Shea. With you."

He did? Her mouth parted, her response on the tip of her tongue. "I—"

"Vincent." Elizabeth's voice penetrated above the buzz of voices and chaos around them. "I've got something."

The world sped up, throwing her back into the present, back into the safe house filled with Blackhawk operatives and Vincent's former commanding officer doing everything in their power to recover her son. Had Elizabeth found a location? Shea pulled out of his grip, heading straight for the network analyst, but couldn't ignore the rush of pleasure rolling through her. He wanted a future with her. "What do you have?"

"Since Lieutenant Richards has been tracking these guys for a few months, she's helped me narrow down a list of possible locations the organization might be using as stash houses." Elizabeth spun the laptop toward Shea as Vincent stepped in beside her. The picture zoomed out to show a map of the city with five circles pinned across the screen.

"Each of these locations has been used as a drop point for the cash and drugs Grillo's runners collect off the streets. Runners go in with the goods, come out empty-handed." Lara tapped each one on the screen. "There's a chance your son is being held in one of these sites."

They had a lead. Her heart threatened to beat out of her chest, pent-up energy telling her she had to go after him now.

"Then we split up." Vincent took the weapon his former commanding officer offered over the table. "And we don't stop searching until we find him."

Chapter Twelve

Shea's strength didn't come from how much she could handle. It came from how she'd survived after she'd already been broken.

Hell, he'd watched her crumble right in front of his eyes, and there hadn't been a damn thing he could do about it but hold her, but she'd held her head high. Only now the cracks had started to show through. She stared out the back passenger-side window as he studied her from the SUV's rearview mirror, a line of tears in her eyes. She hadn't spoken a word since they'd left the safe house, her expression neutral. She'd thrown those invisible walls he'd worked so hard to tear down back into place the minute they'd gotten into the vehicle.

"This is it." Lara Richards pointed to the dominating shadow of the abandoned power plant on the shore of the Hudson River as the sun rose to the east. Two massive smokestacks demanded attention as his former CO shouldered out of the vehicle. Abandoned since 1963, the Glenwood power plant would make the perfect location for Grillo's organization to operate from, but every window from this vantage point remained dark. No sign of fresh tire tracks as he hit the dirt. Nothing to suggest they had the right location, but Vincent wasn't about to give up. Not with Wells's life at stake. Graffiti covered the original red bricks of the building and boards nailed against the windows. "I followed one of Grillo's men here about two weeks ago. He went inside with a fresh stack of cash for a few minutes then came back out empty-handed."

"He didn't notice you were tailing him?" Hard to believe, seeing as how there was nothing but open water, hills of dirt and rock, and few places she could take cover, but it was possible her suspect had only been focused on making the drop. Shipping containers cut off sight lines to one side of the structure. They'd have to go around to access the main entrance. The odor of river algae and something toxic burned his nostrils as he rounded the front of the SUV. His pulse hiked higher as Shea did the same, and he slowed. She hadn't given him an answer—hadn't said anything—since he'd laid it all on the line back at the safe house. They'd risked their lives for each other out there in the wilderness, trusted each other. In a matter of days, she'd become the single most important connection he had to the world, and she'd deserved to know. If she didn't feel the same—if she couldn't because of her past… His stomach jerked. No. He couldn't think about that right now. Getting to Wells. That was all that mattered.

"Must've been in a hurry." Lara hiked her hands to her hips, showing off the Smith & Wesson holstered under her jacket. "Guy never even looked my way before he fishtailed out of here like a bat out of hell."

Dirt kicked up around Shea as she bolted around the sand hill straight ahead of them and disappeared behind a grass-green shipping container.

"Shea, wait!" Vincent ran after her, the wound in his thigh protesting with every step. Dust dived deep into his lungs as he raced to catch up with her, but it was too late. She'd already gained a substantial distance on him, not even looking back toward him as she ripped open the door to the plant. Footsteps pounded behind him as he pumped his legs harder. Lara. They hadn't had time to do a proper perimeter search, to evaluate the risk, to clear the area. Shea could be walking into the middle of a—

The explosion knocked him back with the force of a brick wall headed straight for him at seventy miles an hour. Air crushed from his lungs as the fire and debris engulfed the door where she'd gone inside in an instant. He slammed into the dirt, rolling head over heels, as the all-too-familiar feeling of fire lanced across his exposed skin. A high-pitch ringing filled his ears. He fought to cough up the dirt stuck in his throat and locked his jaw against the pain as he rolled onto his back. Black smoke filled his vision, and the ringing grew louder. Twisting his head back over his shoulder, he searched for her. No. Not her. Vincent put every last bit of strength he had left into getting to his feet. He stumbled forward and hit the dirt again. "Shea!"

Her name growled from his mouth.

The bastards must've known they were coming, must've rigged the explosion to trigger once the door was opened. "Shea!"

"Vincent!" His name barely made it through the ringing in his ears. Lara Richards covered her mouth with one hand as she stumbled toward him coughing. Caked with dirt, her normally blonde hair had darkened considerably, the blood from the laceration across her forehead staining the strands red. She clutched him, nearly tugging him to the ground. He had to get her back to the car. His former CO was alive because she'd been far enough back from the epicenter of the explosion.

But Shea… He searched the massive hole blown into the side of the building. Had she been lucky enough?

He fisted Lara's leather jacket, dragging her to safety. The bullet hole in his shoulder screamed for relief, but he couldn't focus on that right now. Shea. He had to get to Shea. He deposited Lara near their vehicle. Turning back toward the plant, he forced one foot in front of the other. Fire climbed the boarded windows, scarring the bricks of the plant. He raised his uninjured hand to block the heat of the flames from his face. Images of that night— memories—lanced across his brain. The pain, the smell of gasoline, the screams of his team echoing around him. He physically shook his head to shove them into the box he'd kept stored at the back of his mind for so long, but there were too many similarities. The people responsible, the abandoned building. Only this time it wasn't his team in danger. It was his partner, and he wasn't going to lose her. He couldn't. Her son couldn't. "Shea!"

Still no answer.

The high-pitched keening in his ears subsided with every step gained. Ornate brick fell in chunks at the edges of the hole the device had ripped into the side of the building where the door used to be. Humidity hit him in a wave as he hiked through the opening, loose rubble threatening to trip him up. Pools of water and garbage lined the vast atrium that used to hold the plant's turbines. Windows above created a cathedral-like feeling, trapping smoke against the glass. A steel girder fell from the second floor, and Vincent flinched as the combination of metal on cement vibrated through him. She had to be here. There were no other options. Not for him. "Answer me, Freckles."

Another sound broke over the crackling of fire, and he spun around to narrow it to the source. Had it been her? Brick and remnants of the large wooden door she'd gone through piled against the southern wall after the blast, and he vaulted over the mass in order to sift through the rubble. His heart launched into his throat as he spotted a single ash-covered hand among the debris. There. "Shea." Tearing his sling from his injured shoulder, Vincent groaned against the pain as he worked to clear the debris from on top of her. He didn't care how much damage he caused to the muscles and tissues in his arm. He'd take a hundred more bullets if it meant getting to her in time. "Almost there, baby. Hang on."

"Vincent." Her voice came from behind, and every cell in his body awoke with awareness. He twisted around to find her standing at the opposite side of the atrium. Ash clung to her pale skin, eyes shadowed, but there she stood. Unharmed.

Alive. But if she'd gotten enough distance between her and the explosion, who had he been trying to unbury from beneath the rubble? She stepped forward, reaching for him as he maneuvered around the piles of rock and steel to get to her. Relief coursed through him as she buried her head against his chest, his fingers threaded into her hair. She shook her head. "He's not here."

"It's going to be okay. We're going to find him. I promise." He'd already deduced that fact after the effects of the explosion had cleared from his head. Whoever'd taken Wells wouldn't risk harming him until they got what they wanted. Her. In order to hurt him. Pushing her back, he searched her for fresh blood, injuries, anything that contradicted the fact she was standing here, unharmed, after the blast. "How did you get clear from the explosion so fast?"

"It doesn't matter." Her watery green gaze, brighter when surrounded by dark ash and dirt, shifted to the body beneath the rubble. In an instant, she slid her attention back to him, her hand pressed flat over his heart. "Wells is still out there somewhere, and I need to find him." She leaned her cheek into his palm, closing her eyes. "But after what just happened, after everything that's happened over the past few days, you should know I…" His beard bristled as she opened her eyes and trailed a path down toward his chin with one hand, his nerve endings burning. "I want a future with you, too."

His heart skipped a beat. "Really?"

"Yeah." Her nod was all the confirmation he needed. Shea pushed her hair from her face, that brilliant smile tunneling through the nightmare of the last four days and straight into his core. His wounds, the organization they were up against, the case he hadn't been able to solve for over a year, none of it mattered. This, right here. She mattered. There wasn't anything he wouldn't give for her. "I was lost, for a really long time, but working with you on the joint cases these past few months has been the most frustrating and exciting time in my life." Nervous energy played across her expression. "There's something I need to tell you before we decide to give whatever this is between us a chance."

"Shea." He smoothed the pad of his thumb beneath her eyes, ash and dirt smearing across her soft skin. "I don't care what's in your psych eval. I told you before. There's nothing you can do or say to convince me you're not the woman I've gotten to know over these last few months."

Surprise contorted her expression, and she stepped out of his hold. Her mouth parted, eyes narrowing at the edges, and Vincent realized his mistake. Too late. "What did you just say?"

VINCENT HAD ACCESS to her department psych eval? No. Not possible. That information was privileged. In order for him to get his hands on it…

"Blackhawk Security got a copy of my eval." The words left her mouth no louder than a whisper, her voice hollow. "They wanted insurance the officers you'd be working with during the joint investigations were trustworthy or mentally stable, right? Even though all that information falls under doctor-patient confidentiality." The blood drained from her face, gravity pulling her body toward the ash-covered floor. She'd managed to avoid getting blown up after charging through the front door. She'd spotted the explosives around the doorframe and pulled Grillo's man in front of her as a shield before the blast, but right now she felt as though the organization that'd kidnapped her son—that'd tried to kill her—had succeeded. Her stomach soured, bile working up her throat. She shook her head to dislodge the truth. "But this is the kind of thing Blackhawk does, isn't it? You and your team skirt the law when it suits you. Anything to solve the case. Everyone else be damned."

Including her. What had Sullivan Bishop said back at the safe house? That she was one of them, that they protected one another? Rage burned hot and fast in her veins. They protected one another, all right, but she'd never been part of their team.

She'd been a resource, an access point in which to collaborate with Anchorage PD and evaluate sensitive information for investigations. Nothing more. But what hurt more? Vincent had been an integral part the entire time.

"Everything you said is true. Our psychologist vetted the officers we recruited for the task force with the department's permission in case one of our investigations went sideways." He tried to close the distance between them, but she countered his every step. A combination of hurt and surprise contorted his expression, but she didn't have the energy or the motivation to let it affect her. Not anymore. He dropped his shoulders away from his ears, almost as though in defeat. "Yours was one of the evaluations, but Shea, I swear I never read your file."

"I don't believe you. I know exactly the kind of lengths you and your team will go to to get what you want, Vincent. Why should this be any different?" If he hadn't read that file, he wouldn't have known about the one thing that'd kept her from giving herself over to him fully, that'd resurrected her fear of him walking away every time she'd wanted to tell him the truth. Smoke burned her nostrils, sweat building at the base of her spine as the embers continued to consume the plant. Everything inside her ached, head pounding in rhythm to her pulse. She'd trusted him, had started to imagine a future with him, believed him when he'd said he'd never turn his back on her. He'd taken that trust and used it against her. Same as her ex-husband had when she'd found him in bed with his assistant, just before he'd walked away with her son. Same as her family and friends had before deciding she wasn't worthy of their help or love. "Was that why you requested me as your partner all those months ago? Because you thought you could use my mental health in order to leverage me to cooperate?"

He took another step toward her, but this time she held her ground. "What? No. I would never—"

"Don't lie to me." She wouldn't let him see how much it hurt. Instead, Shea gave in to the familiar explosion of rage she'd tried to keep locked away. Anything to help her sever the connection they'd forged over the last few days, to keep herself from admitting how hard she'd fallen for him. The muscles in her jaw ached as she steadied her gaze on his. "How long have you known?"

"I had an idea of what you'd been struggling with that night in the ranger station. You kept trying to convince me you weren't the woman I thought you were, and I didn't want to believe you. Nothing you said lined up with what I saw during our joint investigations." Vincent's voice deepened, his throat working to swallow. "But Kate confirmed it in the hospital when she confronted me about how I feel about you. She said you might not ever be in a position to love me back."

Shock of his admission rolled through her, but she did everything she could to make sure her expression didn't change. He loved her. But that wouldn't alter the fact that she couldn't trust him—or his team—ever again. Her fingernails bit into her palms as loss tore her apart from the inside, a distraction to keep the tears at bay. She'd wasted enough time. Wells was still out there. Alone. Afraid. Clearing her throat, Shea kept her head high when all she wanted to do was sink onto the floor as the power plant collapsed around her. She stepped into him, ignoring the rush of heat his body elicited inside, and drove her hand into his jacket pocket to extract the SUV's keys. She clutched them harder than necessary, forcing herself to stay in the moment, then looked up at him. "Kate was right. I won't ever be in a position to love you, Vincent. Not as long as I can't trust you."

"Shea, don't do this." He locked his hand around her arm. "If you go after Wells alone, they're going to kill you, and I won't be there to stop them. Please. Let us help you find him."

"I've always been alone." That'd been a truth she'd accepted until she'd crash-landed in the middle of the Alaskan wilderness with a forensic technician who'd given her a glimpse of real happiness. But as she'd come to realize too late, it'd been a fantasy all along. She ripped her arm out of his grip, her skin burning where he'd touched her. "Grillo gave me the chance to walk away, and as soon as I recover my son, I'm taking it. I'm sure your team can give you a ride back and help you bring down his organization without me."

Shea maneuvered around him and headed for the hole blasted into the side of the power plant. Tendrils of fire climbed around the edges but not hot enough or dangerous enough to stop her from escaping. The weight of his attention on her back crushed the air from her lungs. The tears fell then, but she wouldn't turn back. There was nothing to go back to. Wrenching the SUV's door open, she caught sight of him positioned where the door she'd gone through used to stand. Heat waves distorted his features, his intensity burning hotter than the flames around him. It must've been difficult for him to charge into that fiery building for her after what'd he'd already been through, but right now, she couldn't let herself care. She climbed inside the vehicle and hit the button to start the engine. Dirt kicked up behind the SUV as she sped from the scene, entirely focused on the road. Elizabeth had messaged them a list of all of the stash houses the network analyst and Lieutenant Lara Richards had narrowed in on as part of Grillo's operation. She'd hit every single location until she found her son.

Lieutenant Richards… Shea hadn't seen Vincent's former CO since she'd breached the power plant. Lifting her foot from the accelerator, she let the SUV slow to a crawl before turning onto the main road that'd take her to the next location. Had there been another operative stationed at the power plant, one who could've gotten to Lara while Vincent had torn Shea's heart from her chest? She hesitated at the thought of turning back around, of facing the man who'd betrayed her after what'd just happened, but Lara deserved better. The lieutenant had helped them every step of the way with the investigation, handed them leads Blackhawk Security wouldn't have been able to find, offered to run testing on the casing she and Vincent had recovered from the warehouse…

Shea stepped on the brakes, her weight shifting forward as the SUV skidded to a stop. Leather protested under her hands as she tightened her grip on the steering wheel. Lara Richards had been at the warehouse last night, arriving within moments of Grillo's men closing in, and shot two corrupt officers with a .38 Smith & Wesson without hesitation. So why hadn't NYPD dispatched homicide detectives or IAB investigators to get her and Vincent's statements about what'd happened? Why hadn't Lara called it in?

Lara's weapon was standard issue for the NYPD, and the lieutenant had admitted to taking a keen interest in the organization's movements over the last few months. To the point she seemed to know more about Grillo's crew than the NYPD did. What if her involvement in the case was more than an attempt to make up for turning her back on Vincent before the fire? He'd theorized the killer who'd shot the four original victims and the IAB officer must've had forensic experience. As a lieutenant, Lara Richards would have authority over Grillo. She could've ordered him and his team to bring down her and Vincent's plane, to take care of loose ends.

Shea swallowed around the tightness in her throat. Only problem was everything running through her head right now would be viewed as circumstantial evidence, but if she was right, Lara Richards had means, opportunity and motive to take out both her and Vincent.

She had to go back. She had to at least explain the possibility to Vincent. Slamming the SUV into Reverse, Shea hooked her arm around the passenger-side headrest. And gasped.

"Hello, Officer Ramsey." Cold metal pressed against her temple as Lieutenant Lara Richards straightened from the second row of seats. Dirt was caked to her leather jacket and jeans, the collar of her white T-shirt underneath crusted with blood from the wound across her forehead. Blonde hair slid over her shoulder as she leaned in closer, close enough for Shea to catch hints of smoke and perfume. "Hand over your sidearm, please."

Her breath sawed in and out of her chest. She shifted her attention to the weapon Vincent had given her back at the safe house, fingers tingling. Could she get to it fast enough? "I should've seen it sooner. You're not investigating Grillo's organization. You *are* Grillo's organization."

"This isn't how or when I wanted to reveal myself, but you and Vincent just wouldn't leave well enough alone. Not even after I tried to have you killed." Lara reached over Shea's shoulder, unholstering the weapon herself, before setting it on the back seat beside her. "No one has gotten as close as you and Vincent. I'd normally take care of the problem myself, as I did with all the others, including IAB Officer Walter, but you have something I want."

The casing. Lara was trying to clean up her own mess. "And you have my son."

"I'll make you a deal." Lieutenant Richards pushed the barrel into Shea's temple, breaking skin. "You tell me where Vincent is keeping the casing he recovered from the warehouse last night, and I'll let you see your son again."

Chapter Thirteen

He didn't know how he was going to win her back, but he sure as hell was wasn't going to lose her. Vincent stepped away from the nearest explosive device, gun in his uninjured hand. Blocks of C-4 had been wired to detonate when triggered above every door and window of the plant. But as far as he could tell, this location had never been used as a stash house or a place Grillo's organization would use to hold a nine-month-old boy hostage. Warning settled between his shoulder blades. One signal. That was all it would take to make it so the best medical examiner in the state couldn't identify his remains, but rigging one of their own places to blow didn't make sense.

Unless it'd been a setup from the beginning.

He bit back the curse on the tip of his tongue. Shea was out there on her own trying to track down her son. He'd screwed up. Even if he hadn't read her department psych eval directly, he'd given her mistrust weight by not telling her his employer had access to it in the first place. She'd trusted him, and all he'd done was prove she was right about him, about his team. Sullivan Bishop had founded Blackhawk to take cases the police couldn't or wouldn't prioritize, asking his operatives to do whatever it took to protect the client. Including skirting the law as Shea had accused. Vincent had solved dozens of cases over the past year by living up to that standard. He'd made a difference he hadn't been able to as an NYPD officer, but in the end, the same principle that'd given him purpose—that had saved so many lives—had driven her away.

She deserved better. Better than him.

She'd survived the worst kind of mental torture he could imagine for a new mother to suffer through, but now, looking back, he understood it wasn't the fact that Blackhawk had access to her psych eval at all. Her desperation to fight for custody of her son, her determination to lose herself in her work, the walls she'd built to keep everyone out. It was all part of the fear that everyone would know—that he would know—how weak, worthless, she'd convinced herself she'd become. But Vincent knew the truth.

Underneath that fear of failure, past her invisible defenses and the guarded expressions, there was a woman who'd never backed down from a challenge, even when she'd lost everything that mattered to her. She was charming, intelligent, authentic and gracious and had more ambition than anyone he'd come across. She wasn't weak. She wasn't worthless. She was everything he'd ever wanted, everything he'd needed to keep him going these past few months. She was…the woman he needed in his life.

She'd brought out the best in him, kept him from isolating himself even further, from losing all contact with the people he cared about in the name of protection. By working at his side, she'd kept him in reality when all he'd focused on the past year was the case that'd almost gotten him killed. He loved her. And it didn't matter if she couldn't love him back. He owed her his life. That would be enough for him.

Vincent moved farther along the atrium floor, kicking rubble and garbage out of his way. Scaffolding lined the walls, an impressive collection of cogs courtesy of the Philadelphia Alfred Box & Co. The crane demanded attention from above, rust and buildup clear from thirty feet below. Grillo's organization might not be holding Wells here, but the officers involved had been here. They'd rigged every entrance and exit with explosives and left a man behind to detonate. It was

Locard's principle. Everyone left a piece of themselves behind and took something with them from a crime scene. Fingerprints, fibers, DNA evidence. Which meant there had to be something here.

This was what he'd been trained to do. Search for the evidence, analyze the scene, find the suspect. He cleared a set of stairs leading up to the second level but slowed. "Evidence."

Holstering his weapon, he pulled the warped casing he'd collected from the warehouse from his jacket pocket. Sunlight reflected off the bronze, even through the plastic evidence bag. He'd left his forensic kit back at the warehouse, but there were other ways to lift prints from evidence in the field. Vincent wound his way back into the atrium and out through a side door facing the Hudson. Collecting a handful of fine dirt, he settled on the edge of an old set of stairs that protested under his weight. A light breeze pushed his hair into his face, his throat burning from the instant drop in temperature. Perfect conditions.

He ripped the adhesive section from the evidence bag, keeping it close, but froze. The second he touched the casing without gloves, it'd be inadmissible in court. Whatever defense attorney would go to bat for these bastards could argue the evidence had been tampered with, and in a case like this, where a large part of the NYPD could possibly be linked to Grillo's organization and charged with a slew of felonies, he'd land behind bars right beside them.

Then again, he wasn't part of the NYPD anymore, and there was nothing he wouldn't do to protect Shea and her son.

He extracted the casing with his index finger and thumb, keeping contact with the metal to a minimum. His shoulder protested as he tried to grip the evidence, but this was the only way to prove what his instincts had been telling him since he and Shea had barely escaped with their lives from the warehouse last night. He picked up the dirt with his free hand and held it above the casing. Then let it go. The wind did exactly as he'd hoped, redirecting most of the sand away from the casing, but the few grains that'd made contact with the bronze clung tight to the oils that whoever'd handled the evidence had left behind. Fingerprint ridges formed in arcs, whorls and loops, but abruptly stopped at one edge as though the print was only a partial.

Just like the fingerprint he'd recovered from the gas can the night of the fire.

Whoever'd loaded this casing into their weapon's magazine and been at that scene the night he'd lost two teammates to the fire. Maybe had even lit the match. The smooth surface of the print on that side meant one thing: whoever'd started the fire that night in the warehouse had burned themselves badly enough they'd lost half of their fingerprint.

His own scars tingled as though remembering what that kind of pain had felt like, which was impossible. He'd lost feeling in almost all the nerve endings in over 30 percent of his injury site. Except when Shea had run her hands over his skin. Hell, he'd never meant to betray her trust. He had to get her back, had to prove he was the one person in this world she'd be able to count on.

But first, he had to bring down the organization Grillo worked for. Dropping the casing inside the evidence bag, he shoved it back into his pocket and retrieved his phone. Every rotation he forced his shoulder to make shot pins and needles down to his fingers, but nothing—not even a gunshot wound—would stop him from getting to Shea. He brought the phone to his ear, and the line connected. "Elizabeth, I need you to send me the location of my SUV and a replacement vehicle to the Glenwood power plant."

Making his way around the side of the building, toward where he'd parked their rental SUV, Vincent scanned the landscape. Where was Lara? He'd left her right here. He dropped the phone away from his ear and spun full circle. No movement. No body.

"Vincent?" Elizabeth's voice barely reached his ears over the rush of wind coming across the river, and he brought the phone back to his ear.

"Yeah, I'm here." Two sets of footprints led away from the plant, but he only recognized one of them belonging to Shea. Dark drops of blood peppered the second set. Had to be Lara. She'd suffered a laceration across her forehead after the explosion. From where the SUV's treads indented the ground, he traced her to the back passenger seat of the vehicle. Confusion rushed through him. Lara wouldn't climb into the back seat in order to catch a ride with Shea. She'd take the front. He gripped the bullet casing in his pocket, the muscles in his jaw ticking with his heartbeat. Something wasn't right. Shea had every reason to get the hell away from him, but Lara? She wouldn't have left him out here without a good reason. "Have you heard anything from Lieutenant Richards or Shea Ramsey?"

"Let me get this straight. You need a replacement SUV because yours suddenly went missing, and you lost both of the officers you took with you?" Keyboard strikes filtered through the line. "I think this is going to put a strain on the relationship Blackhawk has with law enforcement."

He searched the area again to make sure he hadn't missed anything, but there was no sign of either of them. "It's a long story."

"Only Sullivan has checked in. He recovered Bennett at one of the addresses Lieutenant Richards gave us for possible stash house locations," Elizabeth said. "They did a number on him before leaving him to die, but he'll pull through. Autumn is flying in from Anchorage as we speak. Still waiting for Kate and Elliot to call with what they've found at the other two addresses I gave them."

Damn it. Which meant Anthony Harris was still out there. Without him, they might not be able to ID the bastards who'd taken Shea's son. He unclenched his hold from around the evidence bag. Unless... Vincent had already come into contact with the suspect. "I'm going to have to call you back."

He ended the call, studying the footprints in the dirt. Lara's wound hadn't been bad enough that she should've climbed into the back seat of the SUV. Pocketing his phone, he dropped to one knee, his shrapnel wound screaming in protest. He'd recovered the same print from both the gasoline can the night of the fire and the evidence from the warehouse. The suspect had been at both locations, but unless Grillo's organization had been surveilling the murder scene of that IAB officer, which was possible, no one in the NYPD had known Vincent and his teammates were investigating the case on their own. No one except their commanding officer. He scanned the property again. The lack of tire tracks, the explosives... They'd been lured to this location.

His stomach shot into his throat, and he unholstered his weapon with as little contact with the metal as possible. He'd gone to Lara with his theories over a year ago, but she'd shut him down despite the evidence he'd handed over. Solid evidence. Was it possible she hadn't been at the warehouse last night by chance? That'd she'd been waiting for him and Shea all along? That she'd been the one to send Grillo and his team to sabotage their plane? Vincent ran the same test on the barrel of his weapon as he had with the casing, the gun Lara had handed him back at the safe house. Once the dust had settled, the pieces of this murderous puzzle slammed into place. The second print, her middle finger. It was an exact visual match to the others he'd lifted.

Lieutenant Lara Richards was part of the organization bent on killing him.

"Damn it." She'd inserted herself in the investigation to stay a step ahead of them. Now she had Shea in the vehicle with her. He extracted his phone once again and hit redial. The line connected instantly. He didn't bother with small talk. He was running out of time to save the woman he loved and her son. "I know who kidnapped Shea's son, and I know where she's headed."

A GROAN SLIPPED past her lips, waking her from a dreamless unconsciousness. How many times were people going to hit her over the head before her brain decided it'd had enough? Rolling onto her hands at the small of her back, Shea blinked up at the pattern of lights dancing over a white ceiling as the crevices in the floor rubbed against the newest addition to cuts on the back of her head. She'd been restrained in cuffs. Lara… The lieutenant had knocked her unconscious with the butt of her weapon. The floor jerked beneath her, and her entire body slid across the slick surface. Not a floor. The cargo space of a van. The pattern of lights on the ceiling was headlights from oncoming cars.

She struggled against gravity in order to sit up. Keeping out of sight of the rearview mirror in case the driver spotted her through the thick metal mesh separating the driver's cab from the cargo area, she leveraged her boots against one side of the van. She pressed her back against the other and positioned herself behind the driver's seat. She'd always kept a spare handcuff key in her back pocket. If she could reach it, she—

"I know you're awake, Officer Ramsey. I can hear the change in your breathing." That voice. No.

It wasn't possible. She'd watched him sink to the bottom of that lake. "Looking for something?" Officer Charlie Grillo held up a set of handcuff keys for her to see. "As long as you're in those cuffs, I have the chance to pay you back for the damage you and your partner inflicted to my men."

"You couldn't kill me back in Alaska." Every instinct she owned screamed warning for her to get out of the van right then, but when she drove her hands into her back pockets, she only met denim. Shea searched for something—anything—she could use to pry her hands out of the cuffs or as a weapon, but the van had been emptied, presumably to keep her right where Grillo wanted her. She bit back the panic rising, forced herself to keep her voice even. "What makes you think this time will be any different?"

"Because no one is coming to save you this time, Shea." His use of her name—almost intimate—raised the hairs on the back of her neck. "I gave you the chance to walk away back in those woods. You should've taken it."

Those same words echoed in her mind as she thought back to her last moments with Vincent. He'd hurt her far more than Logan had when he'd left, almost as much as it'd hurt when she'd been served with custody papers for Wells. Blackhawk Security had knowingly gotten her psych eval without her knowledge and proven her assumptions about the way Vincent and his team worked. But the worst part? If she was being honest with herself, it wasn't the fact that they'd skirted the law. Vincent alone brought down almost a dozen corrupt cops in those woods to save her life without hesitation and promised to do whatever it took to bring her son home. She hadn't questioned the lengths he'd go to protect her for a single moment.

No. The worst part was he no longer saw her as the woman he'd convinced himself existed, the one she'd desperately wanted to be for him. Strong, full of passion, valuable to their joint investigations, determined, worthy of a man like him. Happy. He'd made her feel as though she had become the center of his entire world, but now that he knew the truth, that she couldn't measure up to the woman he may have built her up to be in his head, it'd be impossible to get that feeling back. No matter how many times he tried to convince himself otherwise, he couldn't love her. He didn't even know her. Not the real her.

The van slowed before taking the next turn, bringing her back into the moment. No windows. Nothing that could tell her where they were without exposing herself to the driver. She closed her eyes against the sudden nausea churning in her stomach. Grillo was supposed to be dead. She had to get out of here. She had to get to Wells. Setting the crown of her head back against the side of the van, she caught sight of wiring framed along the back doors leading into a junction box a few feet away. She forced herself to take a deep breath, then slowly pressed her hands into the floor behind her to scoot toward it. The wires most likely led to the van's brake lights and blinkers. If she could signal the drivers behind them, she might have a chance. She twisted her head toward the driver's cabin as she moved. "Where is my son?"

The moment she got free of these cuffs and escaped, she was going after him.

"Don't worry, Shea. Lieutenant Richards will take good care of your boy." Grillo took a sharp right, pressing her into the frame. "Little guys like that sell for a lot of money nowadays. Plenty of needy couples willing to pay top dollar for a chance at being parents. Think of it this way. We're doing you a favor. He'll have a good life, never knowing you weren't strong enough to take care of him yourself."

"What?" The floor felt as though it'd disappeared out from under her, and even after a few seconds, she couldn't regain her footing. They were going to put her son up for illegal adoption, and she'd never see him again. Blinking against the fog threatening to consume her, Shea pulled at

the cuffs around her wrists until she drew blood.
It trailed down the back of her hands, dripping
from her fingertips. The pain forced her to focus.
No. They weren't going to sell her son to the high-
est bidder. She'd fight for him until she couldn't
stand. She'd sacrifice everything to get him back.
Because she was strong enough, damn it.

Shea worked her palms beneath her glutes, ignoring the strain in her wrists until she was able
to maneuver them to the backs of her thighs. In
seconds, she threaded her feet through the hole
her arms made and brought her hands to the front
of her body. She slid to the breaker box beside the
doors and pried it open. "You read my department
psych eval."

She had to keep him talking, distracted.

"Part of the job. I've seen what depression has
done to a few guys on the force. Most of them
ate their guns at the end, leaving their families
with nothing but debt and anger, but you didn't.
That says something," he said. "You're a good cop,
Ramsey. I think you would've done the NYPD
proud given the chance. Unfortunately, we'll never
find out if that's true."

The van slowed. Grillo was going to finish the
job he'd started back in those woods. Tie up the
loose end. Her.

Adrenaline dumped into her veins. Diving her

hand into the mechanical box, she gripped a white metal lever that would cut power to the vehicle and pressed her feet against the doors as she pulled it back as hard as she could. The metal groaned loud in her ears, then snapped, and she fell back. She didn't have time to pick the lock on the cuffs. The best chance she had in getting to Wells in time was survival. And she'd do whatever it took. Her breathing shallowed as her nerves hiked into overdrive with awareness.

"What the hell?" Grillo hit the brakes.

Momentum threw her deeper into the van, and she slammed against the mesh separating the cargo area from the driver's cabin. He shouldered out of the driver's-side door. The handle. Where had she dropped the handle? She felt along the cold surface of the van's floor but couldn't find it anywhere. The back door was wrenched open, Grillo's dark outline taking up her only escape.

She didn't have time to think—only act.

Shea lunged, tackling her abductor head-on. She hit the dirt and forced him to roll with her but ended on her back with him hovering above. Thrusting her palms into the base of his throat, she knocked him off-balance, then swept the bastard off his feet with both legs, but he recovered faster than she thought possible as she struggled to her feet, still in cuffs. He aimed a fist directly at her face. She dodged the attempt to knock her out, and he launched forward. Hurtling her elbow into his spinal column, she shoved him with her entire body, and Grillo went down. She stood over him, ready to end this once and for all. "You're not taking my son from me."

"We already have, Officer Ramsey," a familiar voice said from behind.

Something hard struck the tendon between her neck and shoulder. She hit the ground, the sound of footsteps loud in her ears as she struggled to get her bearings. A pair of black heels moved into her vision.

"You weren't supposed to be part of this, Shea. So I'm going to give you one last chance before I have Grillo get rid of your body where not even the best forensic investigator in the country could find it." Lieutenant Lara Richards crouched beside her, her rich perfume surrounding her. Clean blonde hair skimmed Shea's face, no sign of blood from the cut on the lieutenant's head. No sign of the cut at all. Had it really been there or had Shea imagined it? Had anything been real? "Where is the casing Vincent recovered from the warehouse?"

Shea twisted her wrists inside the cuffs, half-way sitting up, but the wound in her side wouldn't let her do much more than that. "Go to hell."

A light laugh rolled off Lara's lips, her forearms crossing in front of her body as Grillo got to his feet behind her. "I can see why he likes you so much. You must've been one hell of an investigator to get Vincent's attention. I know how little he lets get to him when he's focused on solving a case." The lieutenant gripped Shea's chin between long fingers, and it took everything inside Shea not to pull away. "Pity for all that talent to go to waste. I could've used someone like you on my side." Lara straightened. "Get her inside. It's time to put an end to this."

Chapter Fourteen

There was only one place this could end.

Vincent pressed his foot down on the accelerator, the momentum pinning him back into the seat. If he was right, Lieutenant Lara Richards wasn't just part of Grillo's organization. She *was* the organization. She'd turned cops into criminals, all while taking a cut along the way, and he hadn't seen it until it was too late. Now she had both Shea and Wells. If his former CO hurt either one of them... Vincent tightened his grip around the steering wheel until his knuckles turned white.

He redialed Shea's number for the tenth—or was it the eleventh?—time. She wasn't going to answer. Not if Lara had gotten to her, but he couldn't stop himself from trying again and again. The SUV's interior filled with her voice as the ringing cut to voice mail, and the tension in his hands drained. Streetlights blurred out the side windows as he sped through the city. "I'm not giving up on you, Freckles. Ever. If you don't believe anything I've said this far, I need you to believe that. I'll be seeing you soon."

He ended the call from the steering wheel and took the next left toward the waterfront. Rain peppered the windshield, the hint of humidity clarifying.

"Five minutes out. Everyone check comms." Sullivan Bishop's orders came through loud and clear from the device in Vincent's ear. The founder and CEO of Blackhawk Security hadn't spent much time in on assignment since proposing to his army prosecutor, Captain Jane Reise, but when it came to the safety of his own people, the former SEAL preferred the field over his massive oak desk.

"Monroe and… Monroe checking in," Kate said over the line, her husband's laugh reaching through the comms.

"Dunham's got your back." An engine growled in the background of Elliot Dunham's earpiece. As much as Vincent hated to admit it, he needed the private investigator's help to recover Shea. He needed all their help. He'd tried solving this case on his own for so long and gotten nowhere. Now he needed his team. "But I'd like to point out, Waylynn is making a bigger sacrifice than all of us by babysitting your demon spawn for this event."

"And there you go ruining the moment." Elizabeth laughed, parent to one of those demon spawn. "Dawson and Levitt checking in."

"Chase in position. I've got eyes on at least two dozen hostile NYPD officers positioned at the west and south sides of the warehouse." The echo of a rifle loading crackled over the channel. Former Criminal Investigation Command special agent Glennon Chase, Anthony Harris's pregnant wife, had jumped at the opportunity to bring down the organization responsible for taking her husband. And if there was one thing Vincent could be certain of tonight when it came to Glennon, she wouldn't fail. Her former partner, newest Blackhawk Security investigator Bennett Spencer, had already been left for dead. She wasn't going to lose anyone else. The woman had fought too long and too hard to keep her small family together.

They all had.

Vincent tapped the earpiece. "Kalani on location." One breath. Two. The weight of the situation settled under his rib cage. He pulled up beside another Blackhawk SUV on the north side of the warehouse and got out, gun in hand. Streetlights highlighted the dozens of officers and squad cars positioned between him and the woman he wanted to spend the rest of his life with. "I owe you guys one."

"I might just be speaking for myself, but we wouldn't mind some of your mom's cooking in exchange for our services," Elliot said.

"Elliot, one more word out of your mouth, and I'll revoke your firearms permit." Sullivan's warning ended the conversation as he climbed from his SUV and stepped to Vincent's side. The former SEAL had seen battle plenty of times and fought a war with his own brother to save his woman. Vincent wouldn't do any less. "You ready for this?"

Within thirty seconds, the rest of his team pulled into the parking lot and took position, each armed and ready for the coming fight on either side of him. Eight Blackhawk operatives up against an entire organization of corrupt NYPD officers. At least two dozen cops studied them from across the street, in addition to the snipers Vincent had no doubt had centered his team in their crosshairs. No one was going to get out of this fight unharmed, but he wouldn't back down. Not this time, and not when it came to Shea and her son. Squaring his shoulders, he strengthened the hold on his weapon. "I am now."

"This is the NYPD," a staticky voice said over a megaphone from one of the patrol vehicles nearby. "Drop your weapons, get on your knees and put your hands behind your heads or we will be forced to take lethal action."

"I don't have a clear visual inside the warehouse. The windows have been boarded," Glennon said from one of the buildings east of their location into their earpieces. "No confirmation on the target's location or if the hostages are inside, but I do have a great view of the two snipers aiming their rifles directly at your heads."

Vincent tapped his earpiece. "No matter what happens, Glennon, I need you to get me inside that building."

"You got it," she said.

Stepping forward, he holstered his weapon. There still might be a way out of this that didn't include bloodshed. He shouted loud enough for his voice to carry across the street and dug the evidence bag from his pocket to put it on display. "I know you're in there, Lara, and I know what you want. Send out Shea and her son, and we can both walk away from this. Nobody else has to die."

"You expect me to believe you're willing to walk away from your little investigation once I hand them over?" The grouping of officers under her control cleared a path as Lieutenant Lara Richards stepped into view. Her laugh hiked his warning instincts into overdrive. She'd been a good cop once, a good commanding officer. What the hell had gone wrong? Or had he even really known her at all? Her wide smile vanished, that cold gaze steadying on his as she unholstered her service weapon and brought it to her side. "I know you, Vincent. I know what you're capable of, and that even if I let Officer Ramsey and her son go free, you'll never stop coming for me." She brought the gun up and aimed. "You're too good a cop."

"You set the fire that night." He tightened his grip on the evidence bag. "You killed two of your own men to try to cover up your operation."

"I warned you before you went to the warehouse that night this case was going to get you killed." She cocked her head to one side. "You should've listened to your CO."

"And the others? The journalist and her assistant, the rookie, the defense attorney and IAB Officer Walter. They were getting too close, right? They suspected your organization was turning the NYPD into nothing more than a hit squad for hire, and you couldn't let them find out the truth." Everything was starting to make sense. "You were willing to risk everything to keep yourself in power, but you made a mistake." He held up the casing discarded after Lara shooting Officer Walters center mass, and lines deepened around the edges of her eyes. He'd questioned the motive behind the shooter leaving evidence at the warehouse scene, but now it made perfect sense. It hadn't been used to keep him and Shea in that building longer after all. "You did the dirty work yourself, but you handed off the cleanup to someone else. And now it's going to cost you."

Lara lowered her weapon, closed her stance as she straightened. "Kill them and pry that casing from his cold, dead hand if you have to."

Gunfire exploded from inside the warehouse, the crack of thunder loud in his ears. Blood pooled in his lower body, cementing him in place. "Shea."

The first bullet sliced across the skin of Vincent's injured arm as Lara's men closed ranks around her. He took cover behind the driver's-side door of his SUV and pulled the trigger. The officer who'd shot at him hit the ground as the rest of the Blackhawk Security team took position and returned fire. Adrenaline coursed through him and sharpened his senses. He tapped his earpiece. "Glennon, get me inside that warehouse. Now."

"Snipers neutralized." The former CID special agent fired again. "I'll clear you a path between the first and second cruisers straight ahead of your position." The sound of rifle shots ricocheted off the surrounding buildings, and Glennon's targets collapsed. Lieutenant Richards's men shouted, crouching behind their vehicles as they searched the rooftops. One called into the radio strapped to his shoulder, but Vincent doubted the bastards would get an answer. "That's your cue, Kalani. I'll cover you until you're in the building. After that, you're on your own."

"Give 'em hell," Sullivan said. "We've got it handled out here."

"Copy that." Vincent pumped his legs as fast as he could as Glennon kept the path through the two head squad cars positioned in front of the main warehouse door clear. He jumped over an officer who'd collapsed to the pavement, then ducked to avoid the fist of another keen on keeping him from breaching the line. Swinging his elbow back, he slugged the SOB and kept running. Pain in his shoulder and thigh clawed for his attention, but the sound of those gunshots from inside pushed him harder. Fifteen feet. Ten. Another officer closing in hit the ground as Glennon kept her word to get him inside the warehouse. He slammed into the door, the rusted hinges detaching as the wood hit the wall behind it. Every nerve ending in his body caught fire as the scent of charred wood and ash filled his senses.

Gun raised, he hugged the east wall as he heel-toed it toward the area where he and Shea had recovered the bullet casing the night before. Muted gunfire from outside punched through the sound of his own breathing. His heart pounded hard at the base of his skull as he took cover behind a blackened stack of pallets. Craning his head around, he spotted his former CO. "Give it up, Lara. There's nowhere to run."

"Run?" Lara fired at him, splinters of wood exploding over his right shoulder. The growl of an engine filled the warehouse, and he chanced another look around the pallets. Brake lights darkened Lara's outline behind her. "I built this organization from the ground up, Vincent. I'm not going anywhere, but I can't say the same for Shea and her son."

"IT'S OKAY, BABY. I've got you." Shea leaned against Wells as much as she could as she tugged at the cuffs around her wrists. His soft hair tickled the underside of her throat. She set her cheek against his head as his screams filled the back of the van. She couldn't hold him. Not with her hands cuffed to the anchor above her head, and everything inside her screamed that if she could get him into her arms, he'd be okay. They'd both be okay. The sound of gunfire was giving him anxiety, and the fact that he'd been ripped away from her ex-husband wasn't helping. Who Lara's men were fighting off, she had no idea. The police who hadn't bought into the lieutenant's ideals? Blackhawk Security? Vincent?

The cuffs cut deeper into her skin as she used her feet to reach for the diaper bag Grillo had

thrown into the back of the van before slamming
the door in her face, but she had to push the pain
to the back of her mind. The canvas slid across the
van's floor easily but fell to one side and spilled
its contents. His pacifier tumbled from the bag.
She pinched it between both boots and brought
her knees into her chest to drop it beside him. He
clutched it in his tiny hand and brought it to his
mouth, but his tears hadn't dried. "I'm going to
get us out of here. I promise."

The driver's-side door slammed shut, and Grillo
started the van's engine.

No. Sitting up, she tried twisting around to see
out the windshield, but the angle only made the
cuffs cut into her deeper. The gunfire outside had
thinned. No more than a few shots here and there.
Had Lara's organization succeeded? Shea kissed
the top of Wells's head as the van lurched forward.
She caught sight of the white metal handle she'd
pried loose before Grillo had brought her to the
warehouse. He hadn't seen it when he'd thrown
the diaper bag in, and she straightened. "Where
are we going?"

No answer.

A bullet dented a section of the van's back door.
Wells's cries pierced the ringing in her ears again,
and she tried to bring him in closer but couldn't
reach him. She had to get out of these cuffs. Some-

one was still out there, and she found herself wishing it was Vincent. He'd risked his own life for hers. He'd given her a glimpse of real happiness, their cases taking so many layers of hurt and fear away that'd built over the last year. He'd shown her what real strength looked like, and that she could be the woman he'd imagined her being if she only believed it was possible. She wasn't ready to give that up. She wasn't ready to give him up. "Grillo, where are we going?"

"I've got my orders, Ramsey." Darkness fell over the inside of the van as they passed through the warehouse's rolltop door at the north side of the property. The side that faced the water. "And no one is coming to save you or the boy this time."

"What do you mean?" Panic rose in a hot rush. She kicked at the van floor, but her heels only slipped along the surface. "You said you were going to have him adopted. That he'd get to live out the rest of his life with a new family."

"Change of plans," he said, the weight of his responsibility in his words. "Boss doesn't want any evidence left to come back to haunt her."

"No." She pulled at the cuffs as hard as she could, biting back her scream as the metal ripped across her skin. She turned around toward him. "Please, don't do this. Please. You can have me but let him go. He doesn't deserve any of this. He's just a baby—"

The driver's-side door flew open, a rush of salt-tinted air filling the van. Her hair flew in chaos around her face a split second before a hand reached in and pulled Grillo from the driver's seat. His scream was silenced as the van's back tires rolled over something solid. The officer's body? Vincent climbed behind the wheel and slammed his foot on the brakes. Her heart was full enough to burst.

"Vincent!" His tangled mass of hair penetrated through the mesh as he tried the brakes again, but the van didn't slow. Something was wrong, and her stomach sank. Realization hit. Oh, no. "Vincent…"

"Bastard cut the brake lines and disabled the button to take the van out of cruise control. Looks like he was going to ditch the vehicle on the way to the water." He hit the brakes again, a sea of black-ness growing closer over his shoulder out through the windshield. They couldn't swerve surrounded by rows and rows of steel girders, couldn't stop without putting everyone in the van at risk. Vincent half spun toward her. "Shea, I'm going to need you and Wells to brace for impact."

"No! I can't protect him with my hands in the cuffs." Her heart launched into her throat as reality set in. Closing her eyes, she accepted the truth of the situation. He wouldn't have enough time to save them both. Shea set her head back against the metal mesh, then turned her attention to her son. She committed everything about him to memory in the matter of seconds, the way his hair smelled, his big green eyes that matched hers, how his thumbs never properly straightened. Logan would have to make sure the doctor took a look at them when he was older. "I love you. No matter what your dad tells you or what you find out on your own when you get older, please remember that. You're everything, and I will always watch over you."

Calm settled over her then, not the numbness she'd become accustomed to, but something lighter, warmer. These past few days with Vincent had done that. Because of him and the word they'd done together, she knew her son would grow up happy and healthy. The man she loved would keep Wells safe.

Leaning down, she kissed Wells one last time and raised her voice loud enough for Vincent to hear. "When we started working those cases together, it was like I'd been pulled out from beneath a crushing wave. Our investigations were the only thing that got me out of bed most days, but if I'm being honest with myself, part of it was you, too. I wanted to see you, to be around you. When you requested me to work on the task force, you helped get me through the worst year of my life, Vincent. I don't know how, but I know I'll never be able to thank you for that. And it seems unfair for me to ask anything more of you, but, please. You have to get him out of here. Save my son."

Wells's cries filled the inside of the van once again, and she couldn't fight back the tears as the weight of what she was asking drilled straight through her. She was asking him to make the choice to save Wells's life over hers.

"I'm not leaving you. We're all going to walk away from this." Shadowed brown eyes lifted to the rearview mirror. "I give you my word."

"You're good at keeping your word. That's why I know you'll do this for me." The tears fell then, and the pressure that'd been building for so long released. She'd fought like hell to gain some semblance of the woman she'd been before giving birth to her son, but because of Vincent, because of the work they did, she realized she wasn't that woman anymore. She was more self-assured and stronger than ever. And she'd give anything to have her son grow up knowing his mother loved him as much as she did. "I know you'll protect him."

Vincent's voice overwhelmed the drone of the van's engine. They were running out of time.

The dock was coming up so fast. "Shea, what are you—"

She braced herself against the oncoming pain before breaking her right thumb. Her scream filled the cabin, scaring Wells into another round of tears, but she pushed past her urge to comfort him to do the same to her other hand. This time, she bit back the groan and slipped her hands free of the cuffs. Sweeping the metal handle she'd detached from the van's breaker box in to her hand, she wedged it down into the small space between the mesh and the driver's seat and pushed as much of her weight into it as she could. The metal gave way, but not enough to get her son to Vincent. She inserted her uninjured fingers into the slots and pulled with everything she had left. The bolts around the edges of the mesh held tightly to the van's frame, but she'd created a hole big enough to get Wells through. Scooping her son into her arms, she kissed him one last time then handed him off, his small fingers sliding against her palm. "Get him out of here."

The van jerked up over the beginning of the dock. "Shea—"

"Go," she said. "Now!"

"I'm coming back for you." Vincent wedged the driver's-side door open with his foot, those brown eyes she'd loved so much steady on her. In her next breath, he jumped from the vehicle with her son in his arms.

She clutched the metal mesh as she watched her partner and Wells disappear beneath the surface of the water in the van's side mirror. Then she was flying. A sea of black consumed the windshield as the vehicle launched itself over the end of the dock. The impact slammed her against the divider, her fingers automatically tightening in the slots as the cabin slowly filled with water. Her head ached where her face had met metal, slowing her reaction time. She'd saved her son and told Vincent the truth. He'd changed her life, helped her heal in more ways than she could imagine. Wells would know she fought for him and become the mother he'd deserved from the beginning. That was all that mattered.

Murky water seeped through the mesh, and Shea forced herself to stand. She had maybe another two—three—minutes before her remaining oxygen escaped the cargo area, but she wasn't ready to die. Not yet. The van hadn't sunk entirely yet. There was still a chance she could escape. She stared straight up at the back doors of the van. The slick surface and her broken thumbs would make it hard to climb, but as Vincent had made abundantly clear, she'd never backed down from a challenge. Least of all given up. "You can do this."

Wiping her wet hands down her jeans, she used the wheel wells of the back tires for leverage. The water soaked her ankles now and was only filling the van faster. Her boot slipped off the wheel well, threatening to pull her back into the water, but she held on to a bracket that made up the frame of the vehicle with everything she had. Her feet dangled below her, the water climbing higher now. She just had to get to the back doors.

A hard thud reverberated down through the frame, and she forced her head up as one back door of the van swung open. Strong, familiar hands wrapped around her wrists, and she couldn't help but trust he'd carry her weight. Just as he always had. "I told you. We survive together."

Chapter Fifteen

Vincent pulled her from the water after their short swim to shore, careful of her broken thumbs, and into his chest. Red and blue patrol lights swept across her features as she steadied herself on the end of the dock. Long hair trailed over her shoulders as she studied the scene behind him. Sullivan, Kate, Elizabeth, Elliot and Glennon watched her and Vincent's backs as a fresh wave of NYPD officers closed in on the scene, Wells safely held in Elizabeth's arms. In an instant, she stepped out of his hold and reached for her son. The boy was all too eager to see his mother again, a giant four-toothed smile crinkling the edges of his eyes as he reached right back for her. Vincent had protected him as best he could when they'd hit the water, determined to keep his promise to Shea, but that was when his team had arrived. With their help, he'd gotten to her before the van submerged. He could've lost her forever if it hadn't been for the support of the men and women around them.

"Thank you," she said to the team.

Sullivan nodded. "Like I said, we protect our own, Officer Ramsey, and Vincent has made it clear that list includes you."

"Damn right it does." Wrapping one arm around her waist, he reveled in the feel of her body pressed against his, in the strong beat of her heart in her chest. Wells tugged on his beard with another gut-wrenching smile—his mother's smile—and laughed. Not even fazed from their short dive into the river. Vincent couldn't resist the wrap of the little guy's fingers around his thumb. "It's over, Shea. We don't have to run anymore."

"I wouldn't be here without you, without any of you." She turned toward Glennon with Wells wiggling in her arms. Smoothing her hand over his nearly bald head, she readjusted her hold on him with a wince, and Vincent couldn't help but smile at the idea of her being so affectionate with their own babies. If that was what she wanted. After everything she'd been through the past year, hell, even the past five days, he'd understand her hesitation to have another kid…or six. But there were more ways to have children than getting pregnant, and he couldn't wait to see her in action. "But what about Anthony? Were you able to find him?"

Glennon's smile broke through the tension of possibly losing one of the best, most-trusted members of the Blackhawk Security team. "Why don't you see for yourself?"

They piled into Vincent's SUV, Shea and Wells beside him in the back seat. Because there was no way he was going to let either of them go. Not now. Not ever. She'd admitted she'd loved him seconds before the worst moment of his life—watching the van launch off the end of the dock into the river. And he loved her. If Shea gave them the chance, he'd spend the rest of his life ensuring they were happy, and that no one would take them from him again. He slipped his arm around her, bringing both her and Wells into his protective hold. Jade-green eyes raised to his as she relaxed her head back against him, and everything inside him heated.

"Did Grillo…survive?" She stared up at him, the slightest quake in her voice.

"Paramedics didn't get to him in time." But Vincent couldn't gather any sympathy for the bastard. Officer Charlie Grillo had tried to kill the woman he wanted to spend the rest of his life with, along with her son and his team. The NYPD would be better off without a man like him in their ranks. "He'll never touch you again. No one will."

Sullivan maneuvered the SUV back toward the

warehouse where spotlights and a perimeter had been set up by NYPD. The low vibration of the engine through his body urged him to give in to the exhaustion of the past few days, to fall asleep with Shea in his arms, but he knew she'd spend the rest of her life looking over her shoulder if she couldn't confirm the nightmare had really ended. That was just the kind of woman and cop she was. The vehicle stopped beyond the officer rolling out crime-scene tape across the rolltop door where he'd watched Grillo escape with Shea and Wells in the van, and Vincent intertwined his fingers in hers. Tugging her from the vehicle, with Wells on her hip, he held the tape up for her to pass beneath, and they stepped back inside the warehouse where his entire life had changed course.

Orders echoed off the cinder block walls as Shea slowed, her attention focused on the woman in the middle of the room. Cuffed and on her knees, Lieutenant Lara Richards and a dozen surviving officers she'd recruited into her organization waited to be hauled back to the precinct. With Anthony Harris, aviator sunglasses and all, standing watch. "You found him."

"Lara had me pinned down behind those pallets over there while Grillo took off with you and Wells in the van." Vincent motioned to the stack, the memories of those few agonizing seconds where he'd given in to the fear of never seeing her again still so clear. He turned to her, fingers tracing a path over her wet clothing. Hell, he still couldn't believe she was here, standing in front of him as though he hadn't almost lost everything that'd mattered to him. "I didn't think I was going to make it to you in time. I was willing to do anything—and kill anyone—to get you back, but before I pulled the trigger, Anthony caught her by surprise. Without him…" Vincent steeled himself against the emotions rushing through him. "I don't know what I would've done if I'd lost you again, Freckles. I love you. I want to be with you, make babies with you, wake up beside you every morning, even if I have to compete with this guy. I will do anything it takes to keep you two safe." He framed her jaw with one hand. "I should've told you I had access to your department psych eval, but I promise you, I will never keep anything from you again. If you'll just give us a chance. Please."

They were in the middle of a damn crime scene, officers collecting evidence and making arrests around them, but seeing as how that was exactly how he and Shea had met, the location for this conversation couldn't be more perfect.

"Vincent, I don't care about you or your team having access to that damn report. I was surprised, angry, and yeah, I felt betrayed you'd kept the truth from me, but…" Shea closed her eyes, spotlights deepened the shadows under her eyes, and his gut clenched. She shook her head, then lifted that beautiful green gaze to his. "I just… I wanted you to keep believing that I was the woman you admired back in that ranger station, the one you'd requested as your partner all those months ago, and I was worried once you discovered the truth, you wouldn't feel that way about me anymore. So many people have walked out of my life because they didn't understand what was wrong with me. I didn't want to lose you, too."

His heart pounded loud behind his ears. He tried to process her words, over and over in the span of a few short seconds, but shock still coursed through him. The pain in his leg and shoulder, the controlled chaos going on around them, it all disappeared. Until there was only her. Vincent threaded his fingers through her hair. "You're never going to lose me, Shea. I might not understand what you're going through, but I'll do whatever it takes to find out. I'm going to be there for you. I'll go to doctors' appointments, I'll watch Wells when you need a break, I'll cook for you and talk you through your cases. However you need me, I'll be there." He trailed a path down her forearm and slipped his hand into hers. "And if that means Kate was right, that you're not in a position to love me back, I'll respect that. I just want you to be happy."

"Really?" Tears welled in her lower lash line as he nodded. She swiped her tongue across her lips, and she dropped her attention to his T-shirt. A distraction. "You said you wanted to make babies with me, but I don't know if I can do that, Vincent. I don't think I can go through what happened to me after I had Wells again."

"I know," he said. "So we'll adopt if we decide we want those babies. We'll babysit Katrina and Hunter and Kate and Glennon's babies when they get here. We'll have Wells when he's not with Logan, and I will still be the happiest man on this planet because I'll be doing it all with you."

The shadows in her eyes dissipated, and his heart jerked in his chest. "Partners?"

"For the rest of our lives." He pushed wet hair behind her ear.

"That would make me happy." Stepping into him, she set her ear over his heart. Right where she belonged.

"Wells?" Logan Ramsey's voice penetrated through the bubble he and Shea had created in the middle of the crime scene, bringing them back to reality. Shea's ex-husband and his new wife pushed past the perimeter, but Anthony Harris cut them off before they got anywhere close. "Wells!"

"The court date." Her eyes widened, and she fisted his shirt with her unbroken fingers with one hand as she clutched her son with the other. "Vincent, I missed the custody hearing. Logan is going to make sure I never see Wells after this. He's going to take my son away. Maybe for good." Closing her eyes, she smoothed her lips against Wells's forehead, and a sudden calmness unlike anything he'd experienced came over her. She opened her eyes. "But I can't keep him from his father, either. I've lived through that, and I wouldn't wish it on anyone. Not even Logan." Shea maneuvered around him, but Vincent wasn't far behind. "It's okay, Anthony. I've got this."

Vincent nodded at the weapons expert in appreciation as arresting officers hauled Lieutenant Lara Richards to her feet. Blazing blue eyes locked on him before his former commanding officer—and what was left of her crew—was forced into the back of NYPD squad cars. Corruption of justice, murder, attempted murder. The district attorney was going to make himself a hell of a career out of this one. Reaching into his pocket, Vincent pulled the bullet casing he'd recovered and handed it off to one of the officers searching the scene. They were going to need it, and in a few months, Vincent would have to come back to New York City to testify. She'd gone after Shea, after her son, and nearly killed him. He'd make sure the lieutenant got everything coming her way. With Shea, his partner, at his side.

VINCENT SMOOTHED HIS hand across her lower back, but nothing would help her process her ex-husband's words any better. Not even him.

"What do you mean? I came all the way to New York for the hearing." The hollowness she'd fought back for so long threatened to consume her, and she could only hold on to Wells tighter. If this was another way for her ex-husband to get back at her, to punish her even more… "Now you're telling me you've already talked to the judge? Logan, please, I know things haven't been easy between us. I wasn't there when you both needed me, but we can work this out—"

"A team of armed men showed up at the house claiming they worked for some security company, told us we were in danger and whisked us away to a safe house, Shea. Then a bomb exploded in front of us, and a bunch of cops took our son out of my arms. They kidnapped him because of something you got him involved in." Logan Ramsey reached for Wells, and it took everything in her power to hold back. She'd meant what she'd said to Vincent. She wouldn't keep Wells from his father. Her son deserved better than that. He deserved to be happy, and if that meant she couldn't be involved in his life, she'd have to live with that. Logan's new wife slid her hand across his shoulders, and the tension seemed to drain out of the man she'd once planned on spending the rest of her life with. "But the men you sent to protect us, Bennett and Anthony, they told us what you did. They told us you were taking on an entire organization of corrupt police officers to make sure we would be safe. So yes, I talked to the judge about custody. Since I'm his legal guardian, I had him approve a new custody agreement while you were searching for our son." Logan pulled a white envelope from his inner jacket pocket and handed it to her. "It goes into effect immediately."

Her hand shook as she took the thick envelope. Vincent pulled her into his side, the only thing keeping her on her feet. She unfolded the documents, tried to read the small print, but it took a few tries before everything became clear. A flood of surprise rocketed through her, her knees threatening to collapse right out from under her. "You…" She looked up at her ex-husband for confirmation. "You're giving me equal custody?"

"After everything you've done for Wells, after hearing how far you went to protect him, I realized you're not the same woman you were when we left Anchorage. You've changed. You seem…

better. Stronger than before." With a glance toward Vincent, Logan switched their son to his other arm and pulled his wife to his side. "I want Wells to grow up knowing both his parents love him. Even if they're not together. We want you to see him as much as you can. Here in New York or in Anchorage. We can work out the details later. I just needed you to know."

She couldn't think, couldn't breathe. Vincent's hand at her back warmed her straight to the core, and for the first time in so long she was…happy. She'd found love with the man who'd saved her life and had a strong future in line for her son. "Thank you."

With a final nod, Logan Ramsey, Wells and his wife were escorted toward a police cruiser that would most likely take them straight home. After living through the chaos of the last few days, she couldn't blame them for not sticking around. Every cell in her entire body wanted to collapse into bed and try to forget the feeling of almost losing her son, the panic. Of almost losing her partner.

"Let's get those thumbs looked at." Vincent led her toward one of the many ambulances parked outside the perimeter of the scene as police worked to clean up Lieutenant Richards's mess. Dozens of bodies littered the ground from an apparent shoot-out, but the Blackhawk Security team—

Sullivan, Elizabeth, Kate, Elliot, Glennon, Anthony—looked as though they'd pulled through. Leaning against their vehicles, they watched as NYPD processed the scene.

Whatever they'd done, however many laws they'd broken in the process, she owed them her gratitude. She let EMTs examine her thumbs and the back of her head where Lara had struck her, all the while trying to keep Vincent from lunging when she groaned from them resetting the bones. As the investigating officers took their statements, Shea couldn't keep herself from touching him as he settled beside her on the back of the ambulance. Just as she'd done in that cave after their plane had gone down. She'd known then she'd fall for him, this intense, protective and thoughtful man. It was inevitable, but she had the feeling it wouldn't end here. It'd be the forever kind of fall. The investigating officer returned to processing his scene, and Shea rested her head against Vincent's shoulder.

"Well, we managed to bring down an entire organization of corrupt cops and solve five cold cases, Officer Ramsey. I'd say we make a pretty great team when we get along." His mouth pressed against the top of her head, his warm breath fighting to chase back the bone-deep cold of the river. He slid his hand up her throat and tipped her head back. He closed the distance between them and pressed his mouth to hers, and everything around them disappeared. The red and blue patrol lights, the fact that his team stood nearby, the crime scene techs. None of it mattered right then. He pulled back enough to speak against her lips. "So does this mean we get to keep working joint investigations together when we get back to Anchorage?"

She couldn't help but smile at the idea. He was right. They did make a great team, and she couldn't wait to see what kinds of investigations they'd be partnered on next. Over the course of the last few days he'd become more than her partner. He'd become her protector, her everything. "Not if it means spending nights in caves, outrunning avalanches or nearly drowning in the back of a van."

"I think we'll survive." Vincent's laugh rumbled through her before he kissed her again. "Somehow we always do."

* * * * *

The wind whipped off the lake, its chilly tentacles snaking into his thin black jacket, which he gathered at the neck with one raw hand, stiff with the cold. His other hand dipped into his pocket, his fingers curling around the handle of the gun.

His eyes darted toward the dark, glassy water and the rowboat bobbing against the shore before he stepped onto the road...and behind his prey.

She hobbled ahead of him, her shoes crunching the gravel, her body tilted to one side as she gripped her heavy cargo, which swung back and forth, occasionally banging against her leg.

A baby. Nobody said nothing about a baby.

He took a few steps after her and the sound of his boots grinding into the gravel seemed to echo through the still night. He froze.

When her footsteps faltered, he veered back into the reeds and sand bordering the lake. He couldn't have her spotting him and running off. What would she do with the baby? She couldn't run carrying a car seat. He'd hauled one of those things before with his niece inside and it was no picnic, even though Mindy was just a little thing.

He crept on silent feet, covering three or four steps to her one until he was almost parallel with her. Close enough to hear her singing some Christmas lullaby. Close enough to hear that baby gurgle a response.

The chill in the air stung his nose and he wiped the back of his hand across it. He licked his chapped lips.

Nobody said nothing about a baby.

The girl stopped, her pretty voice dying out, the car seat swinging next to her, the toys hooked onto the handle swaying and clacking. She turned on the toes of her low-heeled boots and peered at the road behind her, the whites of her eyes visible in the dark.

But he wasn't on the road no more.

He stepped onto the gravel from the brush that had been concealing him. Her head jerked in his direction. Her mouth formed a surprised O, but her eyes knew.

When he leveled his weapon at her, she didn't even try to run. Her knees dipped as she placed the car seat on the ground next to her feet.

She huffed out a sigh that carried two words. "My baby."

He growled. "I ain't gonna hurt the baby."

Then he shot her through the chest.

Don't miss Rookie Instincts *by Carol Ericson,*
available November 2020 wherever
Harlequin Intrigue books and ebooks are sold.

Harlequin.com

Get 4 FREE REWARDS!

We'll send you 2 FREE Books plus 2 FREE Mystery Gifts.

WHAT SHE DID
BARB HAN
LARGER PRINT

HOSTILE PURSUIT
JUNO RUSHDAN
LARGER PRINT

Harlequin Intrigue books are action-packed stories that will keep you on the edge of your seat. Solve the crime and deliver justice at all costs.

FREE Value Over **$20**

YES! Please send me 2 FREE Harlequin Intrigue novels and my 2 FREE gifts (gifts are worth about $10 retail). After receiving them, if I don't wish to receive any more books, I can return the shipping statement marked "cancel." If I don't cancel, I will receive 6 brand-new novels every month and be billed just $4.99 each for the regular-print edition or $5.99 each for the larger-print edition in the U.S., or $5.74 each for the regular-print edition or $6.49 each for the larger-print edition in Canada. That's a savings of at least 12% off the cover price! It's quite a bargain! Shipping and handling is just 50¢ per book in the U.S. and $1.25 per book in Canada.* I understand that accepting the 2 free books and gifts places me under no obligation to buy anything. I can always return a shipment and cancel at any time. The free books and gifts are mine to keep no matter what I decide.

Choose one: ☐ **Harlequin Intrigue**
Regular-Print
(182/382 HDN GNXC)

☐ **Harlequin Intrigue**
Larger-Print
(199/399 HDN GNXC)

Name (please print)

Address   Apt. #

City   State/Province   Zip/Postal Code

Email: Please check this box ☐ if you would like to receive newsletters and promotional emails from Harlequin Enterprises ULC and its affiliates. You can unsubscribe anytime.

Mail to the **Reader Service:**
IN U.S.A.: P.O. Box 1341, Buffalo, NY 14240-8531
IN CANADA: P.O. Box 603, Fort Erie, Ontario L2A 5X3

Want to try 2 free books from another series! Call 1-800-873-8635 or visit www.ReaderService.com.
